Pack of Dorks

BETH VRABEL

SKY PONY PRESS
NEW YORK

To Jon, Emma, and Benny

The Library of Congress has cataloged the hardcover as follows:
Vrabel, Beth.
  Pack of dorks / Beth Vrabel.
     pages cm
  Summary: Propelled from coolest to lamest after trying to kiss Tom Lemmings, Lucy tries to navigate the social hierarchy of fourth grade.
  ISBN 978-1-62914-623-2 (hardback)
  [1. Interpersonal relations--Fiction. 2. Friendship--Fiction. 3. Bullying--Fiction. 4. Schools--Fiction.] I. Title.
  PZ7.V9838Pac 2014
  [Fic]--dc23
                          2014021035

Chapter One

This was the biggest recess of my life.

Today, I would become—officially—the bravest, most daring, and by far the most mature fourth-grader at Autumn Grove Intermediate School.

Today, as soon as that bell rang, I was on my way to becoming a legend.

Today, I was going to kiss Tom Lemming.

Here's the plan: The whole class will run outside. Tom will head straight to the ball shed with Henry. Becky and I will check and double check that Ms. Drake and Mr. Peverell aren't paying attention. Then we'll sneak behind the shed, too.

And then . . . the kiss! Me and Tom. Becky and Henry.

Five minutes. I stared at the back of Tom's red ears from my seat in the middle of the room. When he's excited or nervous, his whole face turns red. It's really cute. (Actually, honestly, it's sort of weird-looking.) Beside me, Becky bounced in her seat, her red curls springing along with her. She thrust her hand toward me, and I automatically reached out to grab the note. But it was Chapstick instead, cherry flavored. My best friend is brilliant!

Becky narrowed her eyes at me until I smeared on some Chapstick and handed the tube back to her. Then she went back to bouncing.

Ms. Drake crossed her arms at the front of the room, glaring at each student in turn, her skinny neck stretched forward like a turtle. "What's going on?" she snapped. "You're all squirming more than the students I taught during the Great Lice Infestation of 1994."

Ms. Drake talks about the year when more than half her students got lice a lot. Like every couple of days, she reminds us not to borrow hats and to never bring a hairbrush to school.

Someone giggled, probably April Chester who giggles all the time. Well, anytime she's not digging in her nose for a booger, that is. She eats them. It's disgusting.

"Something is definitely up." Ms. Drake stood behind her desk.

"How long until recess, Ms. Drake?" Sheldon asked.

"So, recess, huh?" Ms. Drake's eyes narrowed, and she stared us down again. Now she looked more like an eagle than a turtle. "You're all unusually excited for recess."

Silence. The whole class knew about The Kiss. If anyone told, I would die. I mean it. Right there on my seat, I'd turn into liquid Lucy and be a puddle of embarrassment on the floor. I'd die having never been kissed.

The bell rang!

"I'll see you all outside!" Ms. Drake called. It sounded like a warning.

As soon as my penny loafers touched the asphalt, I scanned the crowd for Tom. I caught a glimpse of him and Henry as they ducked behind the ball shed. Step one: Complete.

And now for Becky and me. I clung to her hand, which meant I was bouncing along with her, though my brown hair flopped instead of bounced. Becky's lips were goopy with too much cherry Chapstick. I hastily licked my lips clean, then swiped my jacket sleeve across my mouth. Who wants to kiss goopy lips?

"We should've gone there first," Becky whined. "Ms. Drake is on to us. We're doomed."

"We're not doomed." I rolled my eyes. "We're fine. We just need . . . a distraction." I chewed on my lip for a second, until I realized bloody lips were even worse for kissing than slobbery ones. "Distraction, distraction, distraction," I muttered.

April stood a few feet away, holding a jump rope limply in her hands. Her mouth hung open a little and she sniffed back something horrible in her nose. I fought off a shudder. "Um, hi!" I called to her.

She glanced behind her and back to me. Becky rolled her eyes. April closed her mouth, but didn't answer. We sort of stared at each other a minute, then she said, "Are you going to kiss Tom Lemming today?"

"Yeah," I said. My heart hammered. "But, um, I really need help. You know, from someone trustworthy and smart. Thought of you right away." Sometimes I am such a good liar it scares me.

April's face lit up. "Really? Like how? How do you need help with the kissing?"

"Ew," I said automatically. Becky giggled again. "I don't

need help with the kissing! I need help getting to the kissing without Ms. Drake spotting us. Can you, I don't know, distract her for me?"

April cocked her head to the side and stared at me down her long shiny nose. "Okay." Then she opened her mouth as wide as it could go and screamed. She sounded like a dying cat.

"That'll work!" I yelled, and her mouth stretched into a weird screaming smile.

Becky and I raced down the hill toward the ball shed. A group of fourth graders already was gathered around the sides of the shed. Some people were running up the hill because of the screaming, but anyone who was anyone in fourth grade didn't budge. Tom was waiting for me back there. To kiss me.

I noticed that none of the other couples in class stood together around the ball shed. They were too busy carefully ignoring each other, I guess. I rolled my eyes just thinking about it. I could never be part of such an immature relationship. And then I got a flash of Becky's goopy lips. Was I ready for such a mature relationship, though?

Suddenly my stomach hurt, like the time I ate bad pasta salad at the family reunion. "Becky, I don't know if I want to do this." I stopped, dragging Becky to a halt, too, even though we were still a couple feet from the back of the shed.

Becky fluffed her hair. It fell in long thick curls and she was always separating them. Otherwise she ended up with four huge corkscrews instead of lots of little ones. She smeared on more cherry Chapstick. Her lips looked gloppy and huge. How had I never noticed her enormous mouth before? Did Tom have a huge mouth, too? I stood on tiptoes and tried peeking over Becky's shoulder. I couldn't see Tom's lips, just that his face was red as a stop sign. Would his fat lips smoother my entire mouth? Becky rolled her eyes, almost like she could hear me thinking.

"I don't think we should do this," I whispered again.

"You are *so* doing this," she snapped. For all the bouncing and giggling, Becky could be pretty fierce. She turned the full force of her angry eyes on me. "Remember when you decided penny loafers were cool, so I bought a pair, too?"

"Yeah," I said slowly. After Becky and I wore our new shoes to school at the beginning of the year, every girl in our class now sported a pair.

"Well, I never thought they were cool. But I still wear them. Every day." She leaned in close. "You are going to do this *for me*."

"I don't want to anymore," I whispered. "Let's just call it off."

Becky crossed her arms and rolled her eyes all at once, like she was talking to the stupidest person alive. Maybe she was. "If you want to be popular—and *my* best friend—you sometimes have to do things you don't want to do."

"Why should I?" I blurted.

She glared at me, her cheeks flushing. "It's what separates *us* from *them*." Becky jerked her thumb to the clusters of kids waiting to see The Kiss.

Becky marched ahead, the crowd parting like she was some kind of queen. I followed behind her. It was the first time I followed her. April still was screaming.

Becky strutted over to Henry, who had pushed back his ball cap in preparation for The Kiss. She turned around, waiting for me to strut up to Tom, who stood with his back against the shed. The whole crowd hushed, like they do when the teacher flips the lights.

Becky glared at me now, since I still hadn't walked toward Tom. Her mouth crumpled into a line and then she, weirdly, giggled even though her eyes were fierce. The sound rattled around in my head, but I was relieved to hear something other than my own heartbeat going crazy. I took a step toward Tom, and everyone around us almost hummed. He dropped his arms.

In the background, April's screeching suddenly stopped. It was now or never.

I leaned in to Tom. Just as I was about to touch his lips with mine, I got this super weird image. It was of a raw chicken breast, all peachy and wet, just before Mom dipped it in bread crumbs. My stomach rolled, and I felt a burp, smelly and gross, bubble. Quick as a clap, I pressed my lips against his, careful not to breathe. When I backed up, Tom was smiling, but not at me. He was smiling at everyone else, his fists raised like he had just made a soccer goal.

Someone in the crowd hooted, and Tom's smile grew two sizes. But then he followed the crowd's eyes to Becky and Henry. Becky held Henry's shoulders, and her mouth was still shoved against his. It looked like he couldn't breathe; his whole face was smooched against hers and his eyes were huge and panicky looking. Finally, with a sound like a suction cup being yanked free, Becky backed off. Everyone clapped, and Becky beamed. She fluffed her hair again. All around me, I heard people whispering her name. Not mine. Not Tom's.

Tom crossed his arms.

I let out my breath (okay, my *burp*) in a slow push, like I was blowing up a balloon. It was over. This kissing thing was *so* overrated. So, why was my heart still hammering?

Henry stumbled over toward us, his face still red. He nudged Tom with his elbow, and then they both reached into their pants pockets. They had rings, the kind that you can squeeze to fit onto your finger, with a tiny diamond in the middle. I've seen them at the Dollar General, right next to the register, for two dollars. I know Mom says they aren't real diamonds, but I don't see the difference. Even in the shadowy sunlight behind the ball shed, the small stone sparkled just as much as the diamond Mom wore on her finger. (Well, actually, now she wore it on a chain around her neck since her fingers are so fat.)

Tom handed his ring to me, but still didn't look at my face. I pulled it onto my suddenly sweaty finger and squeezed it to fit. The wiry band scratched the skin between my fingers. "Thanks," I whispered.

All around us, other fourth graders giggled, gasped, or hooted. Tom nodded. Beside us, Becky flexed her fingers to watch the ring catch the light. Then she leaned forward and pecked Henry on the cheek. The crowd went nutso. Tom glanced at me, but my stubborn legs wouldn't step forward. My lips wouldn't pucker. He crossed his arms again.

After what felt like a year or two of standing there, not looking at each other, listening to everyone whisper about Becky, the bell rang. Usually Tom walked with me back to class; it was one of the things that made us so special. Every other so-called couple barely looked at each other, let alone walked back to class after recess so close that their hands brushed. But today, after this most important recess ever, Tom seemed to be gulped by the crowd of other fourth graders and carried away with them back to Ms. Drake's classroom.

Becky threw an arm around my shoulder as I stood there, watching the back of Tom's head disappear ahead of me. "Wasn't that *amazing*?" she said loudly. She yanked her arm tight across my neck so she could make her ring sparkle in the sunlight.

"Amazing," I muttered.

Becky giggled again. Her Chapstick was smeared on her upper lip, making it look like she had a runny nose. "You know everyone wants to be us now. Everyone," Becky whispered. "With these rings, we are the most awesome girls in the school."

I shrugged, trying to shake the raw chicken lips image out of my mind. Becky's eyes were super bright, like our diamonds reflected in them. "Who cares?" I muttered.

Becky wrapped her arm tighter around me, whipping me around until we were practically nose to nose. "Who cares?" she repeated. "Everyone. Everyone wants to be popular. Do you have any idea what I had to do to get here?"

I slowly shook my head. I realized I didn't really know her super well after all. She moved to Autumn Grove last year and never talked about her old school. For the first week or so she was here, I thought she'd be another quiet kid like Sam Righter, who never speaks to anyone and just floats from class to class like a ghost. But one day she showed up wearing a shirt just like the one I had worn the day before, and we started talking. Turns out, she said she loved all the same stuff I did—music, shows, people. And then we were best friends.

"What are you talking about?" I asked slowly, suddenly not sure I was going to like what she said. "People are either cool or they aren't. You can't make it happen."

Becky's Chapstick-thick lips were so close to my ear that her whisper sounded like a shout. "What do you know? You've always been popular. That's why I picked you to be my best friend. I was a dork once. And I'm never ever going to be one again." She fluffed her curls. "And this ring proves it."

I squeezed my fingers together until the ring pinched my skin. "You were a dork?" I sort of laughed. The idea of Becky being like April? It was crazy.

Becky glared at me. "You don't know what it's like," she whisper-shouted again. "Everyone laughing at you. Worse, everyone ignoring you. Being alone. You would do anything—anything—to make it stop."

"Why would it happen to me?" I asked, still confused. "And what do you mean *anything*?"

Becky smiled, but her eyes stayed crazy bright. She shrugged. The second bell rang, meaning we only had a few seconds to get to class. She squeezed my shoulder and marched ahead. Again, I followed her.

Chapter Two

Mom was home.

Mom was never there when I got home from school. This was usually the time I had with Dad, just the two of us. Sometimes we'd go for a walk, never with any place in mind, just head out the door to wherever our feet took us. Sometimes, I'd come home and the whole kitchen countertop would be covered with ingredients that we'd whip into what Mom called "DDs": "Daddy's Delights." Once that meant shrimp with oranges, pistachios, and jam. I ate every crunchy, sweet bite. Sometimes, we'd watch the news, and then Dad would point out the countries the newscasters talked about on the big world map taped to the cement wall in the basement. The whole time, I would talk, talk, talk. I told Dad all about Tom and how we were going to get married right after college and have three children (two girls and a boy). I told him about April picking her nose and about the time Sheldon threw up spaghetti all over the cafeteria and how he really needs to do a better job of chewing his food. And Dad would listen without really listening, just sort of murmuring at things I said, so I knew it would never get to Mom.

Mom tended to make issues. Like once I told her that during lunchtime, Amanda Frankston, who's always super angry, kicked a hot dog when it fell out of its bun. It flew across the cafeteria and hit me in the face. Mom was on the phone with Ms. Drake five minutes later, asking about lunchtime supervision and consequences for kicking hot dogs. She never even gave me a chance to explain that Amanda Frankston is horrible to everyone. It wasn't like she was trying to hit me with the hot dog. She was just kicking a hot dog. Dad would've laughed and never paused in chopping an onion or looking for Sarajevo on the map.

It's probably something to do with the baby, I told myself. I have a habit of talking to myself inside my head. Sometimes I even realize I'm thinking things such as "we need to work harder on math." I mean, who does that? Who talks to themselves in the plural like that? Aside from us, of course.

But anyway, Mom was probably home because of another doctor's appointment. I went along with her to one of them. She thought it would be a good thing to prepare me "for the birth." It was just a regular doctor's appointment, except that the doctor also listened to the baby's heartbeat and did a lot of weighing and measuring. The room smelled like a dirty diaper. I guess that helped prepare me. Pretty soon our house would smell like a dirty diaper.

I tried to get out of going to her other appointments. It's not that I didn't care; I was pretty excited about having a baby sister. But everyone kept talking about me being a "built in babysitter." Which pretty much stinks. I mean, we're not even allowed to be home by ourselves, but everyone thinks we should be responsible for a baby! Seriously?

Plus, Mom has about a million appointments a week. She's high risk, since she's so old. She had me when she was twenty-eight, and now she's nearly forty. Dad keeps calling the baby "the little surprise."

I think a baby is a pretty big surprise.

Mom stood at the kitchen table, her hands splayed across the shiny wooden top and her shoulders pitched high next to her ears. Dad sat in a chair beside her, his hand in the middle of her back. "Eight minutes since the last one," he said. "I'll grab the bag. We can leave a note for Lucy to go to the neighbor's until your mom can pick her up."

"Not yet," Mom muttered. Her shoulders slowly lowered again. "Wait for Lucy."

"I'm right here," I chirped, suddenly scared.

Mom didn't turn around, and her voice sounded too high-pitched. "Hey, honey. How was school?"

"I got kissed." My hands flew to my mouth, trying to cram the words back inside. Dad's mouth popped open with a little *puff*. But Mom, she laughed. An actual, real laugh. Her laugh cut off to a sharp gasp and she grabbed her huge basketball belly.

"Five minutes since the last one," Dad barked. He jumped to his feet. "We've got to go now!"

"We'll—*huff*—talk about—*huff-huff*—that kiss soon." Mom put a hand to my cheek. It was cold and wet. "Right now, we're about to have a baby."

"Now?"

She nodded.

"Should I pack my bag? Am I spending the night at Grandma's?"

"No time!" Dad yelled. He grabbed my shoulder and turned me back to the door. "We're going! Now!"

We weren't having a baby. *Mom* was having a baby. Dad was watching her have a baby. I was sitting in an odd little waiting room outside the section of the hospital where moms have the babies. Behind me were glass double doors locked tight. I could see nurses and doctors dashing around inside the section where I wasn't allowed. Dad said I just had to wait here in this stupid little room with stiff, plastic-y couches next to a fat, ugly security guard until Grandma got here to take me home. Grandma had "just one more hand" of poker and then she'd be here.

Grandma, I should let you know, isn't like other grandmas. She doesn't bake cookies; she rips open Oreos and only eats the fluff. Most of the time when I'm at her dark city apartment, she's on her little metal balcony (which Mom calls a fire escape) smoking long skinny cigarettes. She doesn't wear little pantsuits and aprons like most grandmas. Nope, my grandma wears long, shapeless, tie-dyed dresses that skim the top of her thick leathery feet. She only wears flip-flops, even in the middle of winter. Her kinky curly hair is about thirty different shades of red, orange, gray, and black. Her eyebrows are thicker than wooly caterpillars and her small green eyes are smudges behind her thick plastic glasses. My grandma doesn't give me hugs; she reads my palm and tells me not to walk under ladders.

The only time Grandma ever yelled at me was when I put a loaf of bread away upside down ("Bad luck! Bad luck!"). And I had the best day of my life at Grandma's when we spent all day throwing mugs, vases, and cups against her brick fireplace so she could make a mosaic later.

"Did you ever make that mosaic?" I asked an hour later when Grandma rushed into the waiting room.

"What?" she asked. Her head jerked toward me, like she was surprised I'd be there. I guess my question was a little out of the blue, but why did she look annoyed that I was there? Wasn't she here to pick me up?

Grandma puffed up her chest and squinted her smudgy eyes at me and then peered at her cell phone, cupped in her hand. It vibrated and beeped with a text message. She sighed and didn't look at me again. "Lucy, I'll be right back."

"What do you mean?" I jumped up. "You're supposed to take me home."

Grandma still didn't look at me. She put a heavy hand on my shoulder and gently pushed me back onto the sticky couch. "Something happened. I need to see your mom. Be back soon."

The security guard pushed a little button and the double doors opened. "Can I come?" I yelled after her, but the doors closed behind her. I stuck out my tongue at the security guard, but he didn't even look up from his crossword puzzle.

A nurse must've given me a blanket, because when I woke up a few hours later I was covered in the thin white cloth. Grandma stood over me, her glasses clasped in her hand and her eyes red. She rubbed them with the heel of her other hand. "Come on," she said. "Come meet your little sister."

"She was born!" I jumped up, the blanket falling to the floor. "She's here?"

Grandma nodded, but didn't smile.

"Is Mom all right?" My stomach gurgled, but I don't think it was because no one remembered to give me dinner.

Grandma nodded but still didn't smile. "She's fine. She's going to be fine."

The guard pushed the button and the double doors opened. This time, I got to go through.

Thousands of questions—does she look like me? how big is she? what's her name? what color is her hair? does she have hair?—trickled up to my throat, but I didn't let any of them out. Grandma was moving so slowly, like she was suddenly old, and I found I couldn't speak. The hall was so bright, so white, and the nurses rushed all over the place even though most of the patient rooms were dark. At the end of the hall, light spilled out from a room. I heard a cry; it reminded me of kittens that squeaked all day long for milk. *That's our sister*, I thought. *We're a big sister now!*

And suddenly I was running. First I saw Dad, sitting in a corner, arms folded and eyes shut. Mom sat on a bed, her arms rocking slowly with a wrapped-up white-blanketed lump in her arms.

"Is that her?" I asked and my hands clapped. There was a monster bottle of instant hand wash on the wall, so I slipped off my diamond ring, put it on top of the bottle, and scrubbed my hands with the smelly sauce. See how mature being a big sister made me? No one even had to tell me to wash my hands.

"Can I see her?" I asked when no one spoke, even to congratulate me on making a good decision of disinfecting my hands.

Mom's bottom lip shook, and she nodded. Way too slowly she lowered the lump on to her legs. She pulled back a corner of the blanket. And there she was! My sister, her face like a squashed-up tomato, her lips quivering just like Mom's, and her hair messy brown fluff like mine.

"Hello there," I whispered. "I'm your big sister." I kissed the top of her forehead, and it was so much sweeter than kissing Tom. I thought only of how soft her head was, like pressing my lips to a stack of clean tissues, and how she smelled like baby wash. Clean and new.

"She's perfect," I whispered. "My perfect little sister. Can I hold her?"

Mom let out a weird noise, a crashy sound like stack of books dropping inside of her. Her shoulders shook, and her face crumpled. Dad rushed forward and grabbed the baby lump from her lap, putting it gently into a bassinet.

"What is it?" I asked, crying, too, even though I didn't know why. "What did I do?"

Grandma's heavy hand was on my shoulder again. "Nothing," she whispered. "You did everything right. Your mom just needs some time." Grandma squared her shoulders and spoke loudly over Mom's sobbing. "I'm taking Lucy home.

We'll see you in the morning." She gently touched the baby lump and turned back to the door.

"But wait!" I cried. "I don't even know her name. What's her name?"

Dad looked over at me, Mom's head stayed buried in his shoulder. "We were thinking Molly."

"Molly," I repeated. I touched her soft head again. "Perfect."

Grandma tugged softly on my shoulder, and we left.

"There's something wrong with the baby." Grandma lowered herself onto the chair across from me at the breakfast table the next morning.

"Molly." I licked some jam off my finger. Grandma burnt the toast, so I was smearing about an inch of marmalade over the blackened top. My heart thumped a little, but mostly I felt relieved. Finally, she was talking. The whole way home from the hospital, she barely spoke and then turned on the TV as soon as we got back to her apartment. I watched *SpongeBob* until I fell asleep while she stayed out on the fire escape with her cigarettes and cell phone. "Is that why Mom wouldn't let me hold her?"

"No, that wasn't why." Grandma put both elbows on the table and leaned in toward me. "I'm not sure if your parents want me to be the one to tell you, but it's obvious that something's up and you're not an idiot . . ." For some reason, Grandma's face flushed almost purple when she said idiot. Believe me, I've heard her say much worse.

"What is it?" I asked.

"Did you notice how her face looks a little different than yours?" asked Grandma, her eyes squarely on mine.

"She's just squished looking from being crammed up inside Mom for a couple months."

Grandma nodded. "But that's not all. It looks like Molly was born with something called Down syndrome. Have you heard of it?"

I nodded, thinking of a girl in the grade ahead of me. She smiled all the time, and her face was round. Her nose was flat against her face. She didn't talk much and spent recess on the swings. "She's . . ." I couldn't think of the word for it. Grandma couldn't seem to, either.

"It's a form of mental retardation. It means it's going to be harder for Molly to do things, to understand and learn things, than most people. She's going to have some other . . .

issues, too, probably," Grandma said after a long time of being quiet again. "Like her heart. It was built differently."

"Retardation? Like retarded? But she's okay, right? I mean, she's going to be okay?"

Grandma nodded. "She's okay. She's fine. She's just . . ."

"Different," I finished.

Everything was different.   Mom and Molly were ready to come home on Monday, and Dad said I had to skip school so we could have a day as a whole "family unit" (which made me think of robots). But, of course, Dad only said I had to skip school when I came out of my bedroom at 8:12 a.m. The bus picks me up at 8:15. He was asleep on the couch, the TV blaring away. I don't think he moved since we got home late Sunday night. We went to the hospital to pick Mom and Molly up at 9 a.m. It was really hard not to stick my tongue out at the security guard again.

The hospital was the first time I got to see Molly since Grandma told me about her being different. She had kept me at her apartment until Dad picked me up that night. We went through the McDonald's drive through and Dad seemed to chew more on his words than his fries.

"It's cool, Dad," I finally told him after he said "Molly . . ." and "the baby . . ." and "your mom and I . . ." about thirteen different times. "Grandma told me all about it. It's cool."

He smiled, but it was a tight, really-working-on-the-pulling-back-of-lips smile. "It's not *cool*, but it is what it is."

We didn't talk any more about it and I, for once, couldn't think of anything to say. But I was sure that once we picked up Mom and Molly from the hospital and we were all home, things would be normal again.

But I must be an idiot after all, because nothing was normal.

For starters, Mom wasn't at all Mom-ish. Like, her eyes were puffier than her stomach, which I thought would've been a lot smaller now that the baby was on the outside. (But Dad said that takes time and not to mention it to Mom that I noticed.) She sat on the couch with a blanket wrapped around her and Molly in a bassinet beside her. Every time Molly made a noise, Mom pulled her close and whispered to her or fed her until she stopped whimpering. Then Dad would change her diaper. Then Mom would cry again.

There is something very, very wrong about seeing a mom cry. They aren't supposed to do that.

Plus, the whole thing was very boring. I knew babies stay like big lumps for a few days. But I thought I'd at least get to play a little bit with her. Yet every time I came anywhere close to Molly with a rattle or a stuffed animal, Mom would tell me to back off. "She's resting," or "Molly is content right now." Dad was looking up stuff on the Internet. Every time I went into his office, he closed the laptop and said he needed time "to research."

I couldn't watch TV because Mom and Molly needed to rest. I had left my library book at school and had nothing to read. The phone was disconnected after it rang nonstop for the first few hours we got back from the hospital. I was bored with a capital B.

A billboard-sized B.

Finally I just sat in the chair across from the couch and stared at Mom and Molly. After a few minutes of this, Mom seemed to realize that one of her daughters was, in fact, not resting or content. She cleared her throat, pulled her frizzy hair back into an ugly ponytail, and said, "So. Someone kissed you."

Somehow I totally forgot about telling her that. I forgot about The Kiss entirely! Friday seemed like a really long time ago. I quickly pulled down my sleeve to cover my left hand, not feeling up to showing that while one kid was just being born, the other had been both kissed and given a diamond. Only my ring wasn't on my finger. In fact, the only thing on my finger was a thin green band of skin where the ring had been.

The ring was gone.

My life was over.

Chapter Three

Dad wouldn't take me back to the hospital for my ring. "No way in the world am I heading back there. Not for anything, especially a plastic ring from a fourth-grade boy."

My face burned. "It's. A. Diamond!"

"Diamond rings don't make girls' fingers turn green."

I stomped my foot and growled. Dad laughed, which made me growl even louder. "Are you farting lollipops again?"

Oh, now I was really mad. Once when I was three years old and in the middle of a huge tantrum, Mom asked me if I was farting lollipops. I was so stunned by the question I had stopped mid-scream. She said the only excuse a person had for an all-out screaming fit was either having a leg fall off or farting a lollipop. Now, whenever she and Dad think I'm acting ridiculous, they ask me if one of those things is happening.

"Please!" I cried. "Please! It's really important to me!" Like that time "Puff, the Magic Dragon" got stuck in my head for three days, Becky's whisper-shout about the ring making sure we stayed popular rang in my ears. If I showed up to school without that ring, who knew what would happen?

"Absolutely not." Dad turned his back to me and lifted the lid of the laptop again.

"If I don't have that ring, Tom might break up with me!"

"Then he didn't really care about you to begin with," Dad said without turning around.

"Dad!"

He punched the words DOWN SYNDROME into Google.

"It's not my fault!" I screamed.

"Of course it's your fault," he answered automatically. "You took off the ring and forgot to put it back on. Who else is to blame for that?"

"No!" I snapped, knowing the words about to spill out of my mouth wouldn't help but not being able to stop them. "That's not what I mean. I mean, it's not my fault Molly's retarded and you're all—"

I couldn't finish, not with Dad jumping to his feet and

storming toward me. Somehow I had never noticed just how big and scary my dad could be. But standing so close in front of me, his face twisted and red, his hands in fists, for the first time ever I worried that maybe I did something, said something, that made my dad hate me.

"Get to your room! Now!" he bellowed. I swear, my hair flew back when he yelled. My dad—he never, ever yelled at me. I was too scared to move. That is, until I saw his red face turn purple. "Go!" he screamed even louder, his arm jerking out to point toward my room down the hall.

I ran, slamming the door behind me. In the living room, Molly screamed and Mom sobbed.

At lunchtime, I figured Dad would come to my door and apologize. He might even have my ring, so overcome with guilt at the way he had treated me that he went straight to the hospital and found it. I would hug him and tell him I loved him and knew he loved me. Everything would be fine, fine, fine.

Only he never came to my door.

I smelled grilled cheese (Dad's specialty, since he adds spinach and uses pepper jack cheese and rye bread), but he never called me to the table. Mom did, patting gently on the door with her knuckle. "Come have some lunch, Lucy."

I walked slowly down the hall, but Dad wasn't at the table. He must've taken his plate with him to the office. And my grilled cheese was just white bread and American cheese.

Mom sat with me, but just picked at the crust of her sandwich. Just as I finished, she cleared her throat. "That word," she said. "That word you used to describe your sister. That's a hateful word. A mean word. It's a word we're not going to use in our house."

"Retarded?" I whispered. Just because I wanted to be sure.

Mom squeezed shut her eyes. "That's the second and last time you'll ever use that word. Do you understand me?"

I nodded. Mom patted my hand. "This is confusing for all of us. When I was pregnant with Molly, all the tests came back normal. That happens sometimes, the doctor said," she whispered and her eyes got wet again. "We knew the statistics, because of my age, but we weren't prepared . . . I mean, is anyone prepared . . ."

I squeezed her hand back. "Mom, about my ring—"

"Lucy," Mom snapped. "Forget about your stupid ring."

"My ring isn't stupid. Why can you use that word? Isn't that a mean word?"

Mom's eyes narrowed and dried up. "Back to your room," she said in her quiet, scary voice.

Maybe by dinnertime they'd realize what jerks they were.

Sometimes your parents don't realize they're jerks. Sometimes you even wonder if maybe, just maybe, *you* might actually be the jerk. I heard the radio click on in the kitchen. That's Dad's first signal that he's about to start cooking. For some reason, that one little click made me feel sorry. I should be in the kitchen, part of our robot unit. I shouldn't be alone in my bedroom while my brand-new sister gets cuddles from everyone but me. I should be talking to my dad, not scared that he doesn't like me. Of course he likes me. What's not to like? So I took a deep breath and skipped down the hall.

"Hey, Daddy-o," I said.

He looked up from his cookbook, eyebrows raised. I gave him my sorry-I-was-mean-but-now-I'm-sweet smile. He flashed back his glad-to-see-you-and-of-course-I-like-you grin. "I'm feeling creative," he said.

"Oh no!" Mom called from the couch. "Another DD."

Soon we were chowing down on spaghetti with canned clams and chili sauce. Not one of my favorites, but I ate a little of the sauce then switched to buttered noodles. One upside of Mom not being pregnant any more: she didn't insist on a leafy green vegetable with each lunch and dinner.

Mom still was swirling a noodle around her fork when Molly started squeaking from the bassinet. Dad and I jumped up at the same time and laughed. "Since she's already not content and I'm already done eating, could I go to her?" I asked. "Please?"

Mom nodded and warned me to watch Molly's head. I'm not sure why. But I knew from the hospital's big sister class Mom and Dad signed me up for that I had to put one hand behind her neck when I lifted her out of the bassinet and the other under her rump. I held her close to me and sat down on the couch. I knew that Dad was watching me and felt like I had won a prize or something when he and Mom started talking quietly and not barking out what I was doing wrong.

Finally, I had a minute to get to know my new sister. Her bluish gray eyes blinked slowly. Her lashes were blond, like mine, and curled out so far that when she closed her eyes they fell against her cheek. Her mouth was open in a little circle. I laid her against a couch pillow so I had a free hand. She turned her face toward my finger when I brushed her soft cheek.

"Hello, Molly Lump," I whispered. She blinked again. "I'm your big sister. Soon you won't be so lumpy. You'll even be able to move around and stuff. Then you'll need to stay out of my room. But we'll cover that when you're older. You can stay lumpy as long as you want. I'll hold you."

I smelled the top of her head. Not quite as fresh as when she was just washed at the hospital, but still sweet smelling. She whimpered a little so I started talking some more. Her eyes got a little bigger and she stopped squeaking. "You're a great little sister," I told her. "You're going to love our family. Mom gets cranky, but she gives great hugs. Now that she can drink coffee again, I think you'll be in the clear on the cranky front. Dad's a good listener, but not in a going-to-bring-it-up-later sort of way. I'm going to take really great care of you, even though I've already got loads of friends and a boyfriend. No boyfriend for you, though. Not until you're in third grade. That's a rule. I get to make up rules, now that I'm a big sister."

I suddenly realized that Mom and Dad weren't talking any-more. Sure enough, they were both staring at me and Molly. Mom smiled, even though I guessed she had heard me talk about her crankiness. Dad nodded at me, and the sick feeling I had trapped under my ribs since our fight trickled away.

But then Molly made a noise and her little hand shot out. It knocked against my hand and her long, thin fingers latched on. That's when I saw the narrow green band on my ring finger where my diamond ring had been. And that sick feeling shored up all over again.

I realized something as my alarm clock blared in the morning. I missed the most important day of school ever thanks to Molly Lump. The first day back after The Kiss! Tom was sure to rush up to me and ask what had happened. In fact, I bet Ms. Drake's entire class was worried that I had some kissing-related ailment. They were probably so concerned! I wondered if I'd have cards shoved in my desk. Maybe there would even be a banner for me.

Having been absent might be just the distraction necessary to keep people—Tom, especially—from asking me about the ring. Plus, if I wore a really long-sleeve shirt and spent the day with the cuffs covering my fingers, maybe everyone would just assume I was being modest out of respect for all the girls who didn't have boyfriends they kissed and who gave them fancy jewelry.

And maybe Dad could take me to the Dollar General this

week and I could get a new ring. And Tom would never, ever find out that I lost the one he got me.

Maybe my life wasn't over!

Except that everything was just as strange at school as it was at home.

It started on the bus. April sat down next to me. Usually, I get the bench to myself and stretch out. But she just plopped her booger-picking self right next to me. Like that would be all right. I mean, I know she helped me out with the distraction during The Kiss, but that didn't mean we were friends. Especially not bus buds. I glared out the window and tried not to look at her. If she was picking her nose right next to me, I would die.

The next strange thing: Ms. Drake had rearranged desks while I was gone. She does that every month or so, but usually Becky and I are near each other. This time, Becky was right next to Tom. My Tom! And Henry was right behind her. On the whole other side of the room, by the door, so they'd be first out at recess. I was stuck next to the window and pencil sharpener. Even worse, my desk, horribly, was next to April. Again! That must've been why she thought we could sit together on the bus. I was right behind Sam Righter. That wasn't as bad; Sam had brown hair that twisted into curls when it was hot outside. He was tall and his eyes were the color of chocolate. Not that I really saw them that often. Sam has this way of not really looking at anyone. Or talking to anyone. Ever. Even though we had been in school together since kindergarten, I don't think I'd ever heard him speak.

But when I finally found my desk, Sam flashed me a quick smile. He has nice white teeth. Ever since The Kiss, I've been noticing things like teeth and lips more. Tom's teeth are really short. Like maybe they should be in a baby's mouth. But everyone, even Tom Lemming, should have a flaw. Keeps them humble. I'm not sure what my flaw is, though. I'll have to think about it.

Strange thing Number Three: When I flipped open my desk, I was sure I'd find a bunch of cards or at least a note from Becky. But I only had books and pencils inside. I glanced over at Becky, sure she'd be waving or mouthing, "Where were you?" But nothing. She was talking to Tom. My Tom! And she didn't seem to realize I was there. Even though I walked right past her when Ms. Drake showed me where my desk was stationed.

But, you know, whatever. I got a piece of paper from my notebook and wrote: *Becky, my mom had her baby! I'm a big sister! And bad news, don't tell Tom, but I lost my ring! Did I miss anything yesterday?*

I passed it to April, who passed it down the row until it landed on Becky's desk. Ms. Drake was taking lunch orders, so she wasn't even paying attention. Becky fluffed her curls and slowly unfolded the note. Tom was twisted in his seat, still talking to her. Becky huffed and shook her head and then—oh, lollipop farts!—she passed the note to Tom! She didn't even glance over at me. Strange thing Number Four.

"Sorry to hear about you and Tom." Sam half-turned in his seat toward me. If his cheeks weren't pink, I wouldn't have believed the whisper came from him.

"Strange thing Number Five."

"Excuse me?" he asked, now fully turned around.

"What about me and Tom? What are you sorry about?" I shoved my sleeve cuff over my hand even though Tom already knew I lost the ring. What the heck was wrong with Becky? Why didn't anyone make any sense today?

Sam's chocolate eyes narrowed and he titled his head to the side like I was the one not making sense. "That you broke up," he said, super slowly like he was talking to someone who might not speak the same language.

"Broke up!" I screeched.

"Lucy!" Ms. Drake snapped. "Speak to me after class." Becky's giggle rang through the room. And Tom, he was laughing, too. Ms. Drake clapped her hands. "Class! Attention!" And then she started droning on about fractions.

Broke up? Tom and I broke up? What? When? No way.

It took fourteen years at least for recess, even though the stupid clock only ticked through two hours. The bell finally rang, and Becky and Henry and Tom—my Tom!—dashed from their super conveniently located desks out the door and to the playground. And me? I got called to the front of the class for a lecture from Ms. Drake. Life is so not fair.

But Ms. Drake surprised me by not wearing her how-could-you face. Instead, it was a new face. One that I didn't like, but couldn't name yet. It was the face you might make if someone kicked your stomach. Maybe she had bad sausage for breakfast? That happened to Dad once and he made a similar face the whole day. I tried not to breathe through my nose. The bad sausage had some other, stinkier, effects, too.

"Have a seat, Lucy," Ms. Drake said softly.

"Um, okay, Ms. Drake, but I'm really sorry about talking during class. I'll never do it again. I really feel good about you drawing attention to it and know that I've learned my lesson so I'm just going to go straight to recess where I can tell the kids in my class that I'm sorry for my rudeness."

"Sit down, Lucy." Ms. Drake's face popped out of the bad sausage look and more into her you're-really-annoying-me expression. I sat down. "I heard from your mom this morning."

"Ohhh-kay," I said slowly.

"She told me . . . about your sister." Bad sausage face again.

"Yeah, I'm a big sister. That's a good thing." It seemed like I needed to point that out for Ms. Drake, who must never have gotten any baby sisters and didn't know. "Molly's great. I mean, she's mostly a lump. But she's great." I smiled encouragingly for Ms. Drake, hoping to pop her out of bad sausage face again.

Ms. Drake stared at me while a full minute of precious recess time ticked by. Finally, she patted my hand and said, "If you ever want to talk, Lucy . . ."

". . . I'll make sure I don't do it during class!" I finished for her, happy to have this bizarre conversation heading back to familiar ground.

Ms. Drake's mouth popped open and she slowly closed it again. Not wanting to drag this out farther, I jumped out of my seat. "See you after recess, Ms. Drake!"

Chapter Four

I was sure that Becky would be waiting for me by the doors. That's what she always did when Ms. Drake kept me after class. Then we would trail around the playground until Henry and Tom showed up and chased us. We'd play tag until the bell rang. That's what we always did. But she wasn't there.

"Whatcha doing?" April stood in front of me on the playground, holding a jump rope in her hand and her mouth hanging slightly open.

"Have you seen Becky?" I asked her. "I need to talk to her."

"She's not going to talk to you. Want to jump rope?"

I shook my head without looking at her. I saw a flash of red curls near the monkey bars, and took off after them.

"Becky!" I called as I got closer. Tom—my Tom!—was chasing her. The two of them stopped and stood statue still with their backs to me when they heard me.

"Lucy." It was the first time Henry had ever spoken to me. His voice was surprisingly deep. He stood straight in front of me, close enough for me to smell his egg sandwich breath, and crossed his arms. Behind him, Becky and Tom slowly turned around toward me, their arms crossed, too.

All around us, fourth graders stopped what they were doing and stared. It was super quiet, but not the buzzing sort of quiet like behind the ball shed. This was church quiet.

"Henry," I finally replied, when it became obvious Egg Breath wasn't planning on moving out of my way anytime soon. "I need to talk to—"

"They don't want to talk to you."

"What?" I stopped trying to stretch around Henry and fell back on my heels. Henry's face was deep red and his mouth a straight line. He kept glancing around at the other fourth graders creeping slowly in to listen.

"They don't want to talk to you," Henry said again. His voice shook just for a second when he added, "No one likes you. Tom hates you now. You suck at kissing."

The crowd gasped, or maybe it was just me. I didn't want to cry, but suddenly my cheeks were wet. Tom leaned forward and whispered something in Henry's ear. Henry crossed his arms tighter and spat, "He hopes you cry until you die."

Tom made a coughing noise. Henry rolled his eyes a little and mumbled something else.

"What?" I squeaked.

Henry sighed and stared up at the sky. "Tom wants his ring back."

I twisted my jacket sleeve around my hand. "I don't have it any more. He knows that." I seemed only able to speak in squeaks.

"Then you owe me five bucks, too!" Tom yelled.

Becky laughed. For real!

The bell rang and everyone ran inside, except me. I watched my former best friend and the former love of my life run side by side into the school. Becky's fingers were loosely linked with Henry's but all her attention was on Tom. Becky's giggle, fake and stupid and mean, trailed back to my ears.

The school doors slammed shut, but I stayed put. Maybe I *would* cry forever, until I died. Until a river of tears carried me far, far away from this place where diamond rings turn your finger green, where boys you kiss hate you three days later, where best friends laugh when you cry, where parents stop liking you, and where babies are born different.

"Time to go inside, sweetie." Ms. Drake put her hand softly on my shoulder. It wasn't like Grandma's heavy hand. It was light as a bird landing on me, but the touch seemed to burn my skin anyway. Now Ms. Drake was calling me "sweetie." What was this world coming to?

She pressed gently against my shoulder toward the door. She led me straight to the girls' bathroom. "You go on in and splash some cold water on your face before coming back to the classroom."

I splashed so much water on my face that my shirt was wet all the way to the middle of my chest and my bangs were splattered across my forehead. But my eyes weren't red any more. I blotted the damp clothes and face with a handful of brown paper towels and then decided I couldn't wait any more.

Slowly, slowly, slowly I walked down the hall to the class-room. Ms. Drake never stopped talking, but I could feel every single kid's face turn toward me as I walked in. I had to walk past all of the desks to get to my seat. Becky giggled softly and

I heard a "heh, heh" snorty sound I knew was Tom's stupid laugh. He whispered something that sounded a lot like "drool."

"It's water, you moron!" I snapped, a little louder than I probably should've considering I was just in trouble for talking during class. Some people in the class laughed, Ms. Drake slammed her hand down on her desk, and Tom's face turned even redder. Becky rolled her eyes at me.

So, basically, I was the moron, I guess.

I can't tell you what happened the rest of the day, because I honestly don't remember. All I know is that no one talked to me. No one looked at me. No one. At lunch time, I sat by myself at a little table right by the doors. On the bus, even April sat somewhere else. And when I got to the bus stop, for some reason I thought maybe Mom or Dad would be there, since both of them were home with Molly this week. But they weren't. I walked the two blocks home by myself and my cheeks got wet again.

I stepped up to the porch and was about to open the door when I heard Mom singing that Molly was her sunshine, her only sunshine. I dropped my book bag and went to the back-yard. I went all the way to the edge of the yard, where a small stream slashed the line between our yard and the old folks' who lived behind us. The sound of the water really made me have to pee. But I sat by the creek for about an hour until I heard Dad calling my name. I ran up the yard and came into the house, letting the screen door slam behind me.

"Where have you been?" he snapped. "Why were you in the backyard?"

I shrugged. Why did it take him so long to notice?

He handed me the phone. "It's for you. It's Becky."

"Lucy?" Becky's voice was too girly sweet.

I made a choky sound. I was aiming for hello, but whatever.

"Are you okay?" she asked, still in that too-sweet voice.

"No!" I bellowed, my voice finally working right. "I am *not* okay."

She was totally quiet and I almost hung up the phone. "Look. Tom kept saying mean things about you yesterday. You weren't there."

"I know I wasn't there," I snapped. "I was having a baby sister at the time." Behind me, I heard Dad make a choky sound, too, only his sounded a lot like someone trying not to laugh. I stomped down the hall with the phone to my room.

"Well," said Becky, her voice more regular now. "Then everyone started talking about you. I knew you'd want me to find out what they were saying, so I pretended not to like you, too, so I could find out. Then you came back today and I couldn't show them I was your best friend, not after pretending I wasn't, so I just went with it. I'm really sorry."

I took deep breaths through my nose and stared at myself in the mirror over my dresser, trying to understand what Becky was saying. "So, you're still my best friend?"

"Yeah," Becky puffed.

She's my friend. She made a mistake today, but she was calling to tell me sorry. Who needs a stupid boyfriend when you have a best friend, right? Tomorrow things would be better. My eyes got wet again, this time because I suddenly felt so much better.

Stupid eyes.

"But here's the thing," Becky said much too fast. "I'm going to keep pretending not to like you. You know, for you. So we know what people are saying. I'll call you every night and we'll talk about it, but no one can know I'm still your best friend at school, okay?"

I swallowed hard. I tried to understand what this meant.

So, I could either have one friend—Becky—who was only my friend when no one was around. Or, I could have no friends. "Is this because of what you said on Friday? About how you used to be a dork?"

Becky took a long time to answer. "I don't know what you're talking about."

"Remember? You said I didn't understand. You said you'd do anything to be popular," I reminded her, hating how shaky my voice was getting. "Are you doing this so I understand? Because, okay. I get it now."

Becky sighed. Even though I couldn't see her, I knew she was fluffing her curls again. "Look, do you want me to tell you what's going on or not?"

"Yeah," I mumbled.

Becky giggled. "Well, Tom says he doesn't like you because you don't kiss long enough. That's what started everything. And then Henry said he noticed you sometimes walk home from school with April. I told him it's just because she rides the same bus, but still, Henry said April's dorkiness might be contagious. Then Tom started singing this song about being fat and stupid and he worked your name into it. The song was super mean, but sort of funny. And then—"

Molly started wailing, I mean really screaming harder than I thought a lump her size could manage, and blocked out the rest of what Becky was saying. "I've got to go!" I yelled over the screams. "My sister needs me!"

But instead of going to see what Mom's new only sunshine needed, I sat on my bed and cried right along with Molly.

Chapter Five

Finally the world's slowest week ever was ending. I was never really one of those thank-goodness-it's-Friday people, but that was before my boyfriend told me he hates me, my best friend spent all week making fun of me, the only person who talked to me eats boogers, a lumpy sister screamed all night, and here I was eating lunch alone. Even April had someone to sit with, though she did have to listen to Sheldon spout dinosaur facts the whole time. Sheldon is dino obsessed.

I carried my orange plastic tray, watching the mashed potatoes and gravy quiver and the peas getting dangerously close to rolling over their little partition into the Jell-O. I was watching the tray so closely I never even noticed Henry standing in front of me, blocking my way, until my penny loafers had to skid to a stop to avoid tramping on him. Great. Contaminated Jell-O.

These visits from Henry were about as much fun as Becky's nightly phone calls, during which she shared all the ways Tom thought I was stupid and ugly. Henry's visits were at least a little shorter. Every day, the same: "Where's Tom's money?"

Here's the thing: I know five bucks isn't a ton of cash. And if I asked Dad for it, he'd probably fork it over without remembering to ask why I needed it. But for some reason, I couldn't bring myself to ask. So every day Henry asked for the money, and every day I said the same thing: "I don't have it."

"Well, you better get it," Henry snapped. He made a jerking motion toward me, like he was going to tip my lunch tray. I jumped back. And now gravy was on my Jell-O. Fantastic.

"Henry, when did you get to be Tom's sidekick? I mean, isn't Becky supposed to be *your* girlfriend?" I looked toward their table, where Becky was leaning into Tom, whispering something in his ear.

"She *is* my girlfriend!" Henry snapped.

"Not for long," I sing-songed.

Henry's jaw clenched so much I could barely make it out when he grunted, "Ten bucks. On Monday."

"Ten?" I squealed. "You said it was five!"

Henry shrugged. "Well, turns out that ring cost ten dollars."

"That's a dirty lie!" I shouted. "They're only two bucks at the Dollar General."

Ms. Drake's heels clipped across the linoleum. Her arms were crossed and her face was mean.

"Ten dollars," Henry whispered and walked toward my former lunch table, where Tom and Becky now were thumb wrestling.

Ms. Drake stopped in place and waited until Henry sat down to speak. "Everything okay, Lucy?"

"Yeah," I lied. I sighed and sunk into the seat at my pathetic empty table. Ms. Drake stood there a minute, then walked away without saying anything more.

"The turkey looks particularly purple today, doesn't it?" a soft voice murmured just behind me. I whipped around. After gym class, when somehow Tom and Henry's volleyballs kept zooming toward my head, I was on the defensive, I guess. Plus my ears were still ringing with Becky's too-high, too-girly giggle.

But it was just Sam. I couldn't tell if he was smiling or grimacing, and his eyes stayed glued to the disgust-o lunch tray. I slowly turned back around. Great. Now I was getting sympathy smile-grimaces from other solo eaters. I could tell, though, that Sam was still behind me. I whipped around again, and this time his chocolate eyes were square on my face. "What?" I blurted.

Sam stood statue still for a second, then slid his tray next to mine. His Jell-O had stayed edible. "It's just, this is my table." Sam sat down and tilted his seat a little toward me. "I kind of thought you wanted to be alone, so I didn't sit here, but it's been a week. I miss my table."

"I thought it was empty," I blurted again. Later, I thought that might've been a mean thing to say. But seriously, the kid is super quiet. He's easy to overlook. "Sorry. I'll move on."

I started to stand up. Maybe I could hang out in the bath-room until the bell rang. But Sam put his hand around my wrist and pulled me back to my seat. "No, I didn't mean that. It's cool, just . . ." He sighed and shoved his hands through his hair, making the curls flatten. "Volleyball stinks, doesn't it?"

"Like a crap sandwich," I said. It was one of Grandma's favorite sayings, but Mom would've freaked if she heard me say it. "Wait! You have gym with me?" A flash of hurt feelings covered Sam's face for a second. It's an easy face to recognize, since I pretty much see it in the mirror every time I go to the bathroom at school.

Sam stared at his purple turkey.

And just like that, I realized that I'm a jerk. I couldn't think of a single thing to say to Sam, even though he was the first person to be nice to me in about a week. So I just went with saying the first stupid thought that flopped in my head. "I'll give you a dollar to eat the turkey. All of it, even gravy."

I could only see the side of Sam's face, since it was tilted down toward his tray, but the corner of his mouth jumped up. "Promise to carry me to the nurse if I start to convulse?" he asked.

"Well, I don't think I could carry you," I said, flicking peas off my Jell-O. It suddenly seemed salvageable. "But I'll drag you for sure. Until my arms give out."

Sam picked up his fork, stabbed a hunk of turkey, and shot me a grin before opening wide.

"Stop!" I shouted, a bit too loud. I could hear chairs squeaking as people around us turned to stare. "I don't have a dollar," I added in a whisper.

Sam looked thoughtful for a second, then said, "How about a different bet then?"

"Like what?"

"Like if I eat this turkey-ish stuff, you'll . . ."

"What?" I asked.

"I don't know. I've got to think about it."

For some reason, I nodded. In three seconds, the turkey part of his tray was bare. I pointed to a glob of gravy. Sam held his nose, scraped it with a spoon, and slurped it down.

I applauded, ignoring the squeaks of chairs all around when I did. "You should meet my dad," I said, thinking of his DDs. "I think he'd like you."

Sam grinned, gravy making his lips shiny. "Now, your turn," he said.

The bell rang. "Ha!" I said.

"Nah, you're not out of the bet," Sam laughed, but I noticed he was rubbing his stomach. "I just get more time to think about it."

We walked back to class together. I barely heard Tom's stupid snorty laugh or Becky's whispers.

"How long does food poisoning take to be in effect?" Sam asked as he held open our classroom door for me.

"Minutes. Maybe even seconds," I laughed.

"All right, class," Ms. Drake said from behind her desk. Her neck stretched as she glared at each of us in turn. I thought her eyes dug into mine a little longer than anyone else, but I bet everyone felt that way. "We're nearing the start of the last semester. A major part of your grade this year will be determined by an end-of-the-year project that will combine English, social studies, and science. You will be responsible for a ten-page research paper that must have at least three separate sources and a diorama of your topic. Plus, you will need to present your project to the class."

"A dia-what?" April called out.

Ms. Drake looked even more annoyed than usual. "Diorama," she repeated. "A three-dimensional display illustrating your topic of choice. And your topic will be an animal." She pulled a small plastic bucket from behind her desk.

"In this bucket, I have twelve slips of paper with the name of a different animal printed on them. Each of these animals has faced unique challenges and overcame them to varying degrees. Your job will be to learn as much as you can about the animals, figure out their challenges and approaches to those challenges, find out how they live and with whom they live, and compose your report and diorama." This is how Ms.

Drake speaks. Seriously. It took our class like five minutes to translate it in our heads.

Henry's hand shot in the air. Ms. Drake nodded toward him. "So, we have to read about an animal, write a paper about whatever makes its life hard, and then make a diorama?"

"Precisely." Ms. Drake opened her mouth to spout off more stuff, but Sam's hand slowly rose. She looked just as surprised as the rest of us to see him volunteering. Maybe it was turkey poisoning. I ducked in my seat a little, feeling guilty, but he actually did have a question. A good one, too.

"You said you have twelve animals," he said so softly even I had a hard time hearing him and I was right behind his desk. "But there are twenty-four of us. Was that a mistake?"

Ms. Drake shook her head. "No mistake. This will be a group project. You will each select a partner. Choose appropriately; you will need someone with whom you can work well, someone who will uphold his or her part of the research, and someone with whom you can work both in and out of class time to complete this project."

Half the class groaned, the other half cheered. I couldn't help it; I whipped in my seat toward Becky. Surely this would be the end of the pretending-not-to-like-me thing. I mean, who else would she work with?

But Becky was smiling wide with her huge bubble teeth right into Tom's stupid snorty face. Just ahead of Tom, Henry turned in his seat. If I wanted to know what my how-could-you face looked like just then, I could see it in Henry's. He slowly turned back around and swatted Jeffery Daniels on the shoulder until he turned around and agreed to be Henry's partner. When I turned back in my seat, my eyes burning, there was April, an inch from my desk.

"Partners?" she said, holding out a hand for me to shake. Then she pulled back, sneezed in her hand, and held it out again. The cuffs of her sleeve were crusty.

This is what my life has come to—being research partners with a nose picker.

Just then Sam turned in his seat. "Sorry, April," he said. "Lucy's going to be my partner." He smile-grimaced again. Very softly, he added, "I *dare* you."

My smile felt so slow, like my face forgot how to do it quickly. I nodded.

April wandered away, plopping down next to Sheldon. They would be a good pair. Sheldon already was squirming in his seat, blubbering facts about Apatosaurus. Sheldon's weird obsession with dinosaurs goes all the way back to kindergarten. I mean, even in fourth grade, his shoelaces were covered in fake dinosaur tracks and today he was wearing a sweatshirt with a T-Rex. It looked like one of those iron-on things. I hoped for their sakes that Ms. Drake was including extinct species in her bucket.

When Ms. Drake came to our desks, Sam smiled at me and said, "You pick."

For some reason, I was a little nervous. Becky and Tom had gotten leopards, which seemed like a really cool animal. Other pairs had mountain lions, polar bears, seals, penguins, and owls. Sheldon was trying to convince April that their pick of elephants could mean mammoths.

"What if I pick something lame, like earthworms?" I stalled. Ms. Drake was glaring at Amanda, who was yelling at her partner Lily for picking squirrels from the bucket. Of course, Amanda is pretty much angry all the time. It's sort of her defining characteristic.

"Well," Sam said, "the diorama would be easy. I can make awesome play dough worms."

I smiled—twice in one day!—and reached in the bucket.

Don't be donkey! Don't be donkey!

"Wolves," I read, too loudly in my non-worm, non-donkey relief. "We're researching wolves!"

Across the room, Tom let out a howl. Henry barked. Becky giggled.

Stupid wolves.

Chapter Six

"So then, Tom said that it's perfect you have wolves because you're such a dog. And Sam is so pathetic that you're the only person he could pick for a partner, even though no one likes you. And then I said—"

"Becky, I've got to go."

And cry. These after-school I'm-still-your-friend-in-secret calls were not exactly the highlight of my day. I stared at myself in the mirror hanging from the back of my bedroom door. My hair was scraggly and matted. Like a dog.

"But I said that you have some friends," Becky stammered. "I stood up for you. I think if Tom gets a new girlfriend, he'll stop being so busy hating you all the time. And then we can be friends at school again."

I took three really long breaths out of my nose. I noticed Mom doing that a lot when Molly cries and Dad doesn't seem to hear her. But the breaths just made me make strange puffy noises into the phone.

"Lucy?" Becky asked.

"I'm here," I said. "I just . . . I don't like this, Becky. Why can't you be friends with me everywhere?"

"I told you," Becky said. "I am your friend, but I want to know what they're saying about you. Don't you want to know, too?"

"Are you sure it isn't because you think they wouldn't be your friend if you like me, too?" I blurted it out, my heart hammering.

Becky was silent for a long time. I heard her making puffy sounds, too, so I knew she didn't hang up or anything. "Lucy, if you're my real friend, why would you want me to risk having everyone not like me? I mean, I couldn't stop them from not liking you or I totally would have. But why would you want that for me? Maybe we *aren't* friends."

"No, Becky," I whispered. "I'm your friend. Really."

"Are you sure?" Becky said. "I mean, it's not like I have to call you or pretend anymore? Maybe you want to be friends with Sam more. I mean, maybe that's your type of *crowd* now."

"Oh, come on, Becky!" I snapped. "You know I want to be your friend. Just like before."

"Then why don't you do something about it?" Becky snapped right back. "Like, make yourself popular again. Or at least stop hanging out with dorks. Henry might be right. It could be contagious."

"Make myself popular again?" I repeated. "Are you serious?"

She *humpfed* into the phone. "It can be done."

It sounded so simple when she said it. But I remembered her face when she was making her diamond sparkle after The Kiss. I remembered her saying she would do anything—*anything*—to be popular. Was I willing to do whatever it took to get my seat back at Becky's lunch table?

"Can you come over?" I don't know why I said it. I didn't even check with Mom and Dad or anything. But I wanted her to come over, show me for real that she was my friend. And maybe I could catch some coolness.

"I don't know if I can."

"Can you ask? I'll wait while you do." And maybe ask my parents, too.

Becky said she'd be right back. I held the phone and walked into the living room. I had time to look around and see that laundry was pretty much covering the couch. That Mom was asleep beside the laundry, her mouth hanging open and drool dripping out of the corner of it. Dad was holding Molly and clicking through channels with a remote in his other hand. Becky's house, however, was sure to be spotless. Her mom had a housecleaner who scrubbed everything her mom didn't want to touch and everyone always put away their clothes. They didn't even wear shoes in the house.

"Dad, can—?" But Becky was back on the phone before I could even ask if she could come over.

"I can't," she said.

"Did you ask?" I swear, it was like two seconds max that she was gone.

"Of course I asked." She sounded huffy again.

"Can you come over tomorrow?"

"I don't think so."

"Why?" I felt sort of ashamed even as I asked.

But before Becky could answer, the doorbell rang. Molly threw out her arms and legs like she thought Dad was going to drop her and started wailing. Mom popped upright on the couch, drool still on her cheek. Dad patted Molly's back and pointed from me to the door.

"Hang on a sec, Becky," I said and stepped over the baby bouncy thing on the floor toward the door. I threw it open and, just like I needed one more thing to make me feel awesome, there was April.

"It's my birthday!" she shouted as soon as she saw me.

"Who's that?" Becky called in my ear. "Is that person there for you?" She sounded much too surprised.

"I have cake! At my house! It's my favorite color!"

"Green?" I asked without really wanting to know.

April nodded vigorously.

"Lucy!" Becky shouted in my ear. "Is someone there? Who?"

"Yeah. It's a friend." I said friend a little too loudly to Becky, I think, because Becky got super quiet and April's face practically split in half with a smile. "I've got to go, Becky. She invited me over."

After I pushed the button to hang up the phone and April still stood there on the doorstep, I realized I had a huge problem. I either had to go to April's house or lie on the spot in front of my parents. Like I said before, I'm awesome at lying.

But my parents are super awesome at calling out my lies. It was a pickle. A big, green, cake-sized pickle.

"Happy birthday, April," Mom half-yawned. "Of course Lucy can come over."

"Is that your baby sister?" April asked, staring open-mouthed at Molly. Her hands stretched out toward my lumpy baby sister and she started to step over the doorstep. Soon those crusty fingers would touch my perfect sister.

"We've got to go!" I shouted, stepping in front of April. "Got to get to the cake!"

I glanced back at Mom and saw her face flush. Dad looked disappointed. I guess he wanted more time as a family unit or something. "I'll be back soon. Really soon, I think."

Dad nodded and kissed Molly's head, which was odd since I was the one leaving.

April skipped beside me on the way back to her house. At first, that was pretty annoying. I mean, we're in fourth grade. I stopped skipping months ago. Plus, she wasn't really good at it. Her arms kept whapping me in the face and her legs sort of twisted out as she moved. But she laughed the whole time and the sun was shining and I was out of the smells-like-sour-milk house and off the phone with guess-who-hates-you-now Becky. Soon I was skipping, too, if only to show April how it was supposed to be done.

She giggled even harder and soon we were skip racing to her house. It was a tie. Somehow all that flailing gave her freakish speed. We flopped onto the porch swing. From inside the house, I heard tons of squealing, laughter, and music.

"Are you having a lot of people over?" I asked.

April shook her head, still grinning hugely. "Nope! Just you!"

"Then who is inside?" I asked.

"My family!" She opened the door, and wow. People every-where! Kids running up and down stairs, April's dad rushing by with a tray of hamburgers and hot dogs, April's mom blow-ing zerberts on a baby's chubby belly, April's second-to-young-est brother zooming by in a Spider-Man costume.

I realized I had no idea how many brothers or sisters April had even though we had been in school together since preschool. Standing in the foyer, it felt like she must be one of a dozen. Turns out, she has three brothers, all young-er, and an older sister. And they're all pretty normal! Ex-cept for the second-to-youngest brother, who is three. (And

I can't really say for certain about the baby.) Scott's the second-to-youngest's name, but everyone called him Scrappy. While we were eating cake (green frosting, orange insides, surprisingly good), he fell off his chair three times for no apparent reason.

Scrappy sort of made me realize why April only talks in bursts. It's really the only way she could ever be heard. The kid never stops talking. Ever.

"One time I played tennis. Guess what? Some guy at preschool said 'buns.' I told him buns are butts and he laughed. Sometimes I try to lie and I can't. What are the things on roofs that aren't chimneys? I had a nightmare last night."

I realized my mouth was hanging open just like April's.

"I heard you had a baby sister, Lucy," April's mom called across the table when Scrappy paused long enough to swallow a mouthful of cake.

"Yeah, her name's Molly."

April's mom—a frizzy haired, rounder version of April (minus the nose picking)—and her Dad—a skinny, always-grinning taller version of Scrappy (minus the Spider-Man costume)—exchanged a long glance. I knew what was coming next: Some way of poking around at Molly's Down syndrome.

All the relatives who kept stopping by did the same thing.

Sure enough: "And how is your sister . . . progressing?"

"Right now, she's basically a lump," I said.

"Lucy, I'm sure—" But whatever April's mom was sure about Molly Lumps was cut short by Scrappy.

"My favorite color is orange. I'm going to be six someday. I'll be a police when I grow up. And I'm going to live in a barn with cats and a wife."

April's older sister turned up her iPod so loud I could hear the beat even though she had earphones in. The baby whimpered. The brother just younger than April fell asleep at the table.

"You're allergic to cats!" I felt a little proud of April for getting a sentence in, even if it was in her annoying every-thing-with-an-exclamation-point way. "We're all allergic to something!" And, almost like she planned it, she sneezed. Something slimy trickled down from her nose but she sucked it back up and ate more cake. I tried really hard not to shudder.

April's mom nodded toward the sleeping brother. "Looks like the new allergy medicine isn't going to work out," she murmured to April's dad. "Just like April, he's just going to have to suffer through."

Scrappy tugged on my sleeve. "Pirates are for real. Did you know that? One time I bit my tongue and bleeded the color blood. Dogs love me."

My mouth hung open again.

Before I knew it, the sun was setting and the cake was gone. April wanted to skip back to my house, but I told her I wanted to walk instead. She sort of hummed beside me, but I didn't mind. Being out of that super loud house made everything else really quiet.

"I'm sorry I didn't have a present for you," I said.

"That's okay!" April grinned. "I'm happy you came over!"

"Me, too," I said, surprising myself at how much I meant it.

Mom was rocking Molly when I came inside.

"Mom, how long is it going to take Molly to figure out how to talk?" I blurted.

Mom swallowed hard. "It takes most babies about a year to learn a couple words. Molly's likely going to need more time than that."

I sighed and plopped down on the couch. "Thank goodness."

When I looked up, I was surprised to see Mom actually smiling at me. I realized it had been awhile since Mom smiled like that, with her whole face instead of just plastic-y lips, and I couldn't help but smile back.

"April has a baby brother, doesn't she?"

"And a not-so-little brother." I closed my eyes again, my ears still ringing with all the noise from April's house. "Mom? Do you think some people can become cool? Or are some people just meant to be dorks and they can't do anything about it?"

Mom lowered Molly into the bassinet beside the rocker and opened her arms to me. She hadn't held me in months, first because I'm too big for that and second because she didn't have any room with her huge baby stomach. Her belly was still big—just a little deflated—but I sat down right on her lap and she wrapped her arms tight around me.

"What's all this about? Are you okay, Lucy?" She tucked a piece of hair behind my ear and looked me straight in the face.

And I almost told her. Really. I almost told her about Tom hating me and Becky pretending to hate me, too. About stupid wolves and dares from Sam and how April was sort of becoming my friend, too, and how that made a really selfish jerky part of me grumble. I almost told her that I've been collecting change from under couch cushions and the laundry basket because Tom wanted repayment for the diamond ring I lost and now when I run on the playground I sound like Santa's sleigh. But if I actually gave him the money, then he, Henry, and Becky would have absolutely no reason to talk to me at all. I almost told her that I've never, ever been lonelier than I have been the last week. I almost told her that I was ready to do anything—anything at all—to make it stop. I almost told her I wasn't sure she and Dad had room to worry about my problems any more now that they had a whole syndrome to manage. All of these things nearly poured from my mouth onto Mom's lap.

But then Mom's eyes got watery and she added, "It hasn't been easy on any of us, figuring out what Molly's future is going to be like and how to handle her health issues. I mean, even all the Down syndrome stuff aside, her little heart needs to be monitored and . . ." She took a long, deep breath. "Friends popping by to see you. Birthday parties. I want all of that for Molly, too. I know it's really early. I mean she's not even a month old . . . but I just . . ." She sighed again. "I'm sorry, honey. I shouldn't be unloading this junk on you. I'm really sorry."

I put my head on Mom's shoulder and wrapped my other hand behind her neck. Her head rested against the top of my head. "It's all right, Mom," I said. I curled my fingers around the hair at the base of her neck, the way she always did for me when I was sad or sick. "I can take it."

She laughed. "You're stronger than all of us, Lucy. I can't tell you how much your Dad and I appreciate how completely loving and caring you've been to your sister. It feels like you're the only one who hasn't been falling apart lately." She sniffled and squeezed me tighter. "It's going to get easier, Lucy bean. We'll be back to normal in no time."

In that moment, when I was holding Mom more than she was holding me, I made a decision.

I was on my own. I wasn't going to ask them for anything.

Chapter Seven

Molly looked adorable. She wore a little jean skirt with a pink lace ruffle around it and a T-shirt with a pink giraffe. The giraffe's horns popped up at her shoulder. Her tights were hot pink with purple polka dots. She wore little pink ballet slippers even though she can't hold her own head up, let alone stand. Mom fastened a little purple barrette in her fluffy brown hair and sat back to admire her little sunshine as she lay in the middle of Mom and Dad's bed. Mom clapped her hands and Molly blinked.

"Watch Molly a sec, okay, Luc?" Mom said when I accidentally-on-purpose bumped into her back. Not to ask her for anything (such as, random example here, a new skirt, shirt, tights, barrette, or little pink ballet slippers). Just to remind her that I was there, too.

I nodded, not that Mom noticed. She slid by me to the bathroom. I stepped closer to the bed. Molly stared at me, probably realizing this fashionable attire of hers was temporary. I was wearing jeans, a yellow T-shirt with a pinkish ketchup stain in the shape of Florida at the bottom, and dark brown penny loafers, even though it was about 80 degrees outside and everyone else wore sandals. At least Mom didn't notice I wasn't wearing socks. You know, there were loads of times—such as when I looked totally rock star with my black-and-white striped poofy skirt and gray shirt with black bedazzled stars—that I wished Mom wouldn't pay attention to what I was wearing. But right now, when I wanted her to see my too-tight shoes and stained shirt so I wouldn't have to actually ask for new stuff, it really was not at all cool.

With zero warning, my head jerked back. "Hold still," Mom mumbled. She yanked a hairbrush through my hair and had to mumble because she had an elastic band and a bobby pin clenched between her lips. "Did you forget to use conditioner last night? And is this toothpaste? In your hair?"

I nodded, which was the truth. I forgot to use conditioner because I also forgot to wash my hair. Or take a shower. In fact, I didn't take one the day before, either. Plus, I guess I leaned a little far into the sink this morning when I brushed my teeth because a glob of dried up toothpaste was making this hair brushing feel more like my mom was trying to yank out my hair from the roots. I felt the skin around my eyes stretch backward and I squealed, "Ouch!"

And then something amazing happened! Molly's little mouth stretched back, too, and her face transformed from the regular little Molly Lump into the happiest looking baby I've ever seen.

"She's smiling!" Mom yelped. "Molly's smiling!" Again without warning, she yanked the hairbrush through my hair. Again I squealed. And again Molly smiled, even wider than before. I couldn't help smiling back. Mom wrapped her arms around me from behind and squeezed me tight. "You made your sister smile, Lucy!"

"This is so wonderful," Mom murmured, her mouth still full of the elastic band and bobby pin. She swept them from her lips and continued, "Today is Molly's cardiology appointment, and I was so nervous. But now, I just know everything's going to be all right." She kissed the top of my head and squeezed me again. I picked up Molly and held her to my chest, like we were a sandwich. Molly Lumps and Mom were the bread; I was the ham.

"Everything's going to be great," I said. And for a second or two, I really believed it. But then Molly Lumps burped, adding a white Pennsylvania-shaped glob to my shoulder, and Mom poked the top of my head with a bobby pin.

I barely could find Sam behind the enormo pile of wolf books at the library table. "Here's one more, young man," Mrs. Fredericks, the librarian, said as she added another brick-thick book to the stack. Remember how I said my grandma was the opposite of how most grandmas look? Well, Mrs. Fredericks was exactly how grandmas are supposed to look, with curly white hair, a teddy bear cardigan, and a super scary goblin face that twisted if anyone spoke above a whisper.

"Why aren't you at the computer lab?" I whispered as Mrs. Fredericks walked off. "You said you wanted to research. I've been looking for you in the computer lab for a half-hour." Henry tripped me twice as I walked through the aisle, Becky rolled her eyes and elbowed Tom as I passed them, and April kept popping up behind the little cubicles like a groundhog. I shuddered just thinking about the whole experience.

"It's quieter here," Sam whispered. "Plus, I don't think wolves have changed all that much since these books were written."

I glanced around the empty library and had to agree it was a nicer place to study. "Is this where you disappear to all the time?" I asked.

Sam looked up from a picture of a wolf ripping apart a moose or something and raised an eyebrow. "No," he said.

Awkward silence.

I grabbed a book from the pile and cracked it open. "So, what did you find out so far?"

Sam passed his notebook to me. Wow, he was organized! He had numbered facts as he wrote them. I scanned to the bottom. Twenty-five facts. So maybe most people would be like, "Awesome. I have the coolest partner ever who can do all the research and I don't have to do a thing." But most people have, oh, I don't know, lives. I have no life. I was counting on this project to give me a little bit of a distraction. And, fine. I'll be honest. I was hoping to spend a little more time with Sam. He was nice to me (and, still being honest, also nice to look at).

Yet here he was, hiding away in the library with The Goblin bringing him every wolf book ever made and making lists—lists!—of facts. We'd have this project done in no time and I'd be back to Patheticville. I bet Sam wouldn't sit with me at lunch anymore when we weren't partners. He'd probably join the Everyone Hates Lucy Club. Maybe he'd ask to be president. Not that Becky or Tom would let him.

"What's your problem?" he asked. I realized he was staring at me. Well, more precisely, he was staring at the way my hands were crumpling up the list he made.

"I thought this was a *joint* project, Samuel."

"Samuel?" He slowly closed the book. "Why are you mad?"

"Why are you in such a rush to find out everything without me?"

"Because you weren't here. And I was." He actually had the nerve to look confused.

"Because I was in the computer lab! Where *normal* people go to research!"

The Goblin shot us a look, but it had nothing on Sam's angry face. "You're being a complete jerk," he said in a whisper that felt like a yell.

Seems I was bringing out the angry face in lots of people lately. I swallowed hard and looked down at the book so I wouldn't have to see Sam. "Why are you in such a rush to finish this project? I wanted to do some research, too. Together."

I didn't look up, even when Sam pushed the pile of books more to the center of our table, closer to me. "Let's start over then," he said softly.

I nodded.

"But you can't say things like that I'm not normal, okay? I thought we were friends."

We're friends? I smiled, still looking down, and read from the book in front of me. "'Wolves are social animals. They live in groups called packs.'" I finally glanced up at Sam, who was just sitting there, staring at me. "Shouldn't you be writing this down?"

By the end of the hour Ms. Drake had given us for research, I had learned a lot about wolves. First, they aren't a lot like dogs, who just sort of follow what people want them to do. Wolves take care of each other and themselves. Wolf packs, they're really important. Each one has a male and female leader, or alphas, who lead the pack. But everyone in the pack works. They have jobs to do, depending on what they're good at doing—hunting, taking care of the pups, even playing is a job. Everyone depends on everyone else. It made a lot of sense, and made me realize wolves must be pretty smart. Sam and I decided to make a big section of our report all about the different jobs wolves had within the pack. I wondered where I would fit if I were Lucy Wolf. But then Sam started sharing what he was reading about scapegoats. And I didn't have to wonder any more.

"So these wolves, they're the ones all the other wolves love to pick on. So they're usually smaller and weaker than the rest of the pack. They're mostly forced to do stuff alone, like eat after everyone else does or sleep separately while the rest of the pack sort of piles up together," he said. "Sometimes, the rest of the pack bands together and just attacks the scapegoat for no reason."

"They're bullied," I said.

"Right," Sam said. His eyes were really bright; he got into this research stuff. Whenever it was his turn to talk and mine to take notes, I noticed he seemed really excited about what he learned. I guess I was, too, but this scapegoat stuff was depressing. "The rest of the pack bonds over picking on the scapegoat. So, in a way, that's sort of that guy's job."

"Well, that's stupid." I dropped my pencil. I didn't want

to write any more notes about picked-on wolves. Suddenly, I hated wolves.

Sam just shrugged, though. "Yeah, but they're not trying to be mean. It's just the way their world works. Other wolves feel better about themselves—stronger, more capable, more important to the pack—by pointing out who is weaker and less capable."

"Jerks," I muttered. "Do the scapegoats ever fight back? Can they work their way back up to alphas?"

Sam flipped through a couple pages of his book. I caught a glimpse of two big wolves pinning down a third. One had its mouth on the pinned-down wolf's throat. The other was pouncing, his two front legs on the back of the picked-on wolf. No problem guessing which one was the scapegoat, especially since the pinned-down wolf's tail was tucked between his legs while the other ones held theirs high in the air. Jerks.

"Um," Sam said. "Yeah, they can fight back, but it usually ends badly for them. It says here that if scapegoats act aggressively, more pack members join in to sort of prove who's in charge. It looks like if the scapegoat fights back, he gets so beat up he usually leaves the pack."

I chewed my lip, thinking of Lucy Wolf limping off alone.

"Then what?"

"Huh?" Sam asked.

"Then what?" I repeated. "If the scapegoat goes off on his own, can he make his own pack?"

Sam looked at me, startled. "Why would a wolf want to be on its own? I mean, he should just deal with it. Being the scapegoat is a stinky job, but it's still important."

"No. He should go off on his own, form his own pack with other scapegoats, and be awesome." I crossed my arms.

"A pack of scapegoats?" Sam half snorted, half laughed, which reminded me of Tom. I scowled at him. Sam stuck out his tongue, The Goblin shushed us, and we both started to laugh.

We still were laughing when we walked back into Ms. Drake's room. She gave us one of her dragon looks so we tried to pull it together, but when Tom made a sniffy, snorty, snobby noise as we walked by, it set us off all over again.

When I finally made it into my seat, I could hear Becky's whispers and see from the corner of my eye that Tom was glaring at us, but it didn't bother me. Much.

You know how sometimes things aren't really all that funny,

but something about it strikes you as hilarious and so you end up smiling all day about nothing and looking sort of freakish but you can't stop doing it? That's how the rest of my day went.

I had a stupid happy smile plastered to my face all day, even though it meant that Tom, Becky and Henry had to work twice as hard to be jerks. They even got some people who aren't quite popular but not quite dorks to join the Everyone Hates Lucy Club. I guess seeing me happy was to blame for the recruiting effort.

When Amanda Frankston waited in the hallway bus line with her arms tightly crossed and her face grimacing, I didn't think it had anything to do with me. Amanda's always angry, and I was still smiling, imagining a pack of scrawny scapegoat wolves. Plus, I was trying really hard to ignore Henry, who was in the bus line next to us. I angled my body away from him, which also put my back to Amanda. So it took me awhile to tune into her grumbling behind me.

Amanda was about a foot taller and wider than anyone else in fourth grade, and her frizzy, too-thick hair made her head look like a little mushroom on top of a boulder body. She was talking to April, who, when I finally caught on and glanced behind me, looked like a rabbit cornered by a dog. April is tall, but in this stretched-out-taffy thin way. Standing next to Amanda, even April seemed dainty, small, and more than a little scared. While Amanda never had actually broken bones or punched someone's face in, the potential always was there, just under the surface of her too-broad, always-clenched fists.

So there I stood, smiling to myself about imaginary wolves, taking way too long to realize that Henry was laughing in his mean, not-really-funny-actually-just-mean sort of way and everyone in my bus line and his were staring at my stupid smiley face.

Amanda's voice rose. "What's wrong with her hair? That chunk at the top of her pony tail is standing straight up!" Amanda's laugh was meaner than Henry's. "Didn't you know you're supposed to wash *all* your hair, Chunk Head?"

Henry joined in next. "What's all over her shirt? Is that snot?"

"Maybe she forgot to put on clean clothes?" Amanda huffed. "Hey, Chunk Head, wearing jeans that are too small isn't the same as wearing capris!"

I probably should've spouted back a comment about

Amanda's own fashion sense, which was, to put it kindly, challenged. She was wearing black mesh sport shorts and a black T-shirt. At least she matched. And at least her clothes were clean.

I thought of Molly, sweet and smiling this morning in her new outfit. I thought of Mom trying to smooth out my hair but being distracted by Molly smiling. Then I thought of Molly spitting up all over my shirt. For a second, I was so mad. So mad at both of them.

Very softly I heard another voice behind me. "I think her hair's pretty. And I like her T-shirt." I knew how hard it had to be for April to stick up for me. How much easier it would've been not to.

"What do you know? You think boogers are a tasty treat," Amanda practically shouted, and everyone in both lines laughed.

"Yeah," came a nasally, pitchy laugh. "Lucy looks like a Corythosaurus!"

"Shut up, Sheldon," Amanda snapped.

But Sheldon is incapable of not sharing his dino facts, I guess, even when faced with our class' T-Rex. "They're called the helmet lizard, for this fin-like lumpy crest on top of their heads. Their faces are duck-billed and they stood on two legs. Corythosaurus were herbivores and . . ."

Maybe I should've stood up for April the way she had for me, but I couldn't seem to move. Even when the bus pulled up and everyone else got on, I stood there. The driver had to honk his horn before I moved. I took a seat next to April, but she just stared at the window.

Chapter Eight

I trailed a step behind April after we got off the bus, trying to think of a way to thank her for sticking up for me without actually making her think we were friends. I know that's horrible of me and makes me just like Becky, but it's true. If everyone saw that I was friends with April, I'd have zero chances of ever digging my way out of this Tom and Becky thing. I mean, I hadn't figured out how to make myself popular again, but I knew hanging out with April was not the way to do it. Making friends with other residents of Dorkdom would be like settling. It'd be like accepting that this is where I belong.

Still, when April turned left to go home and I kept walking straight to my house, I called out, "Bye, April!"

She didn't even wave.

Great. Now even dorks hated me.

Grandma's old clunker car was in our driveway. The garage door was open, and I could see my mom's van wasn't there.

"What are you doing here?" I asked Grandma as soon as I opened the screen door.

Grandma was sitting on the couch, one ring-heavy hand resting on Molly's belly. "Well, hi, and how do you do to you, too," Grandma snapped. She didn't look up from her book, a paperback with a muscled man holding a fainting woman bulging out of her dress on the cover.

"Okay, fine. Hi, Grandma. How are you? What are you doing here?" I didn't mean to sound so snappy, but I guess a big part of me was hoping to come home and find Dad waiting to go for a walk. I wanted to come home and have something be like it used to be. But then I remembered. Molly's appointment with the heart doctor was today. "Is it Molly? Is her heart all right?"

Grandma put the book down on her lap, bending the spine. She squinted up at me through her smudged glasses. "Molly's fine. I'm more worried about you at the moment."

"The doctor said her heart's okay?" I asked again, still standing in the doorway with my book bag.

"Come in the house and shut the door," Grandma snapped. "Molly's fine. The doctor had good news. It looks like the heart murmur they saw at the hospital when she was born is going to close just fine. Her heart's strong. I told your mom and dad I'd babysit my granddaughters while they went out for dinner to celebrate."

I breathed out slowly. The bricks I didn't know had been piled on my chest dissolved. Molly's heart was fine.

But Grandma still stared at me like she was searching for a tick. "I'm more worried about you," she repeated.

I shrugged off my book bag and plopped onto the couch. "I'm fine. What's for dinner?"

"It's four o'clock, Lucy. Respectable people don't eat dinner until seven." She smiled then and piled a few pillows around Molly like a nest. Then she hoisted herself up. "I'll make some popcorn. You find some chocolate."

We feasted on popcorn and the chocolate Mom had hidden in the cupboard since Easter. It was a little chalky, but still delicious. Grandma's popcorn is the best. It's regular microwave popcorn, with a drizzle of melted Nutella and peanut butter. I felt bad for poor Molly, who woke up to just a bottle of disgust-o milk.

For a long time, the only sound in the living room was the munching of popcorn and the turning of Grandma's paperback pages. I worried about getting chocolate smudges on my library book but figured Sam and I were the only ones who would ever actually check out wolf books from The Goblin and risked it.

"So, what's up with you, squirt?" Grandma asked. I realized I hadn't heard her pages turn or popcorn chewing for a while.

I shrugged.

"Listen," she said, and closed her book. "No one stares at a picture like that without having something bothering them."

I realized my library book was open to the page where the pack is attacking the scapegoat wolf. I sighed. "Things are sort of crappy at school."

"Kids giving you a hard time?" Grandma asked. Her voice was gruff.

I nodded, angry at the way my eyes were about to spill over with tears. I didn't want to cry because of stupid Amanda and stupid Sheldon. And especially not because of even stupider Henry or Tom. And never because of Becky.

Almost like Becky knew I was thinking mean thoughts of her, the phone started ringing with her daily guess-who-hates-you-now call.

"Ignore it," Grandma said. We didn't speak until the phone stopped ringing.

I felt Grandma's heavy hand on top of my head, but just for a second. Then she swiped my popcorn bowl and scooted closer beside me, munching on the few peanut butter-covered kernels that remained. "Kids can be jerks." (Well, she used a different word than jerks. But I'm not allowed to say that word.)

I nodded. "You can say that again."

So she did. I laughed a little, and she smiled wide for a second. Then her hand weighed down my shoulder for a minute and suddenly I was crying.

She let me carry on for a little bit, then said, "The thing is, Lucy, they don't know they're being jerks. And they won't know until they're a lot older. I was the biggest jerk you could imagine when I was your age."

"You were?" Maybe I was surprised at first, but after thinking about it for a bit, it was pretty easy to imagine Grandma as an angry Amanda-like kid.

She nodded. "I made life horrible for a lot of people who didn't deserve it."

"Why?"

Grandma shrugged, sending her beaded necklaces rattling. "Because I could." She sighed. "It made me feel better, stronger, to make other people feel weak." She pointed again at the picture of the scapegoat attack. "I guess it's not all that unusual."

"But it's stupid," I snapped. Just because animals do it, too, doesn't make it okay.

"Absolutely stupid," Grandma agreed. She shifted a little and glanced over at Molly, who was back asleep. "So, how'd they find out?"

"Find out what?" I asked, confused.

"About Molly." Grandma's voice was quiet and gruff again.

Again I felt anger rush through me. "They didn't," I said. "It's not about Molly. Believe it or not, it's about *me*." I slammed shut the book, popped off the couch, and stomped as hard as I could to my room. I didn't even come out when Mom and Dad returned an hour later. I just pretended to be asleep, all through their happy cooing to precious Molly and her whole, healthy heart.

❖ ❖ ❖

"Rise and shine! It's a beautiful day!"

I pulled my blankets over my head and rolled away from my open door and Mom's smiling face. "Go away. It's Saturday."

"A bright, sunshiny Saturday!" I heard her humming down the hallway and soon smelled coffee brewing and bread toasting. I don't like toast, and while coffee might smell good, it tastes like liquid earwax. Or at least how I think liquid ear wax would taste. I've never tasted ear wax, though I guess I could ask April if it tastes like coffee. When her nose is empty, she moves on to her ears. Then I remembered that even April wasn't talking to me at the moment, and I buried myself under my blankets again.

Whoosh! The blankets were rudely yanked back and my window blinds pulled up. Bright sunshine and cold air hit me.

"Huzzah!" Dad yelled. I groaned. "Up and at them, Lucy bean!"

"What is *wrong* with you and Mom today? It's Saturday! The day we sleep in!"

Dad answered with a tickle attack, his fingers tapping the little triangle inside my shoulders and making me laugh even though I was still mad. He's very good at making people laugh when they want to be angry instead. "Your mother and I have made a decision. A decision to be happy! And we're starting today."

"I made no such decision." I yanked the blankets back from the foot of my bed.

"As your parental units, we've decided on your behalf."

"Staying in bed will make me happy." My head fell back in the perfect fluff of my pillow. Now if Dad would just go away.

"Not today! Molly slept for four hours straight last night. A new record! I've never felt so refreshed! We're going to seize the day!"

"Stop yelling!"

"No!" he chirped.

"Grrr!"

"That's the spirit!" Dad clapped his hands and whistled.

With a huge sigh, I sat up and planted my feet on the floor. "Fine," I grumped. "I'm up."

I've got to admit: when I made it to the breakfast table and saw that Mom had arranged orange slices in a flower pattern and Dad had made a smiley face with egg eyes, bacon smile, and a toast triangle nose, I started to catch some of their happiness bug. Not that I'd share that with them yet.

"So," I said, eating the bacon smile first, "now that I'm up, what do we have to do today?"

"Be happy," Mom said simply and sat beside me. She was holding Molly and patted her rump gently. Molly blinked slowly from where she curled against Mom's chest. I leaned over and kissed her nose, and she smiled again. Her smile was pretty awesome.

"Be happy doing what exactly?" I asked, moving on to making my egg face a Cyclops.

"Let's take a walk," Dad said.

"Yes!" I squealed. Finally!

But then Mom said, "Great idea! Let's go to the park. Maybe you'll see some friends there, Lucy."

It took a lot of work to keep that smile on my face. But as much as I wanted to just take my usual wandering walk with Dad, I saw how determined Mom was to be happy and couldn't suggest she and Molly stay home.

"Are you sure?" Dad said softly. "It's T-ball season. I'm sure we'll see a lot of families at the park. Are you . . . ready for that?"

"Yes," Mom said firmly. I wondered what that was about.

I didn't have to wonder for long.

As soon as we got to the park, other moms flocked to Molly's stroller like Sheldon to a dinosaur exhibit. "The baby!" they shrieked in this annoying stretched-out voice. "Aaaahh!"

And then they'd lean in and look at her round little face, at her narrow eyes and her flat nose, and at her pink little mouth and the soft double chin. I didn't understand at first, the face the moms made. I thought maybe Molly had spit up or something, because the moms all reacted the same way. They stopped mid-coo and bit their bottom lips. Their breath left in a wobbly gasp, and they stopped just short of touching Molly. They looked at Mom and their eyes got wet.

At first, Mom kept her decision to be happy. She smiled brightly and said Mom things such as, "She's almost two months old already!" and "Our little sweetie-pie! It's her first time at the park." But the other moms just nodded and said, "How are you doing? How is everyone adjusting?" I could hear Mom's teeth grinding behind her smile.

"What's wrong with them?" I whispered to Dad, who wasn't even trying to be happy any more.

Dad looked at me for a long time, and I didn't think he was ever going to answer. Finally, he knelt so we were eye to eye. "They're noticing that Molly has Down syndrome."

"Oh," I said. "That's it?"

"Yeah," Dad sighed and stood again. "That's it."

"But she's still a baby. I mean, they wanted to see a baby. She's a baby."

Dad stared at me for another minute and then said, "I love you, Lucy." It was one of those times when someone says they love you and you feel it more than hear it.

By the time Mrs. Chester dashed over—April's baby brother stationed on her hip—Mom was losing it. "Let's go," she whispered to Dad.

But Scrappy, wearing a baseball uniform and glove, darted around his mom and ran toward us. "April's friend!" he yelled. I think that meant me. "Hi, April's friend! Are you here to watch me play T-ball?"

He kept right on yelling until he was right beside us. "It's a type of baseball. I'm awesome at it. I might be the best baseballer ever. Is that why you came to the park? Because of how awesome I am at T-ball? Did April tell you?"

Scrappy's brown eyes were so big and so sure and so

stinking happy that I wasn't at all surprised when Dad said, "Yup. That's exactly why we're here."

"Knew it." Scrappy nodded. "Mom," he called over his shoulder to Mrs. Chester. "April's friend and April's friend's parents and April's friend's baby are here to watch me play." He skipped back to the field.

Mrs. Chester laughed as she approached us. "You've absolutely made his day," she said.

Then came the moment we all dreaded. Mrs. Chester leaned over the stroller and looked at our Molly.

"Good morning, precious!" she said, her voice just as happy, just as strong, as before. "It's a pleasure to meet you."

Then she looked at Mom and Dad and said, "Congratulations on your baby girl!"

I looked at Mom. She wasn't working to be happy any more. Dad wrapped his arm around her and squeezed. To Mrs. Chester, he said, "Thank you. That means a lot to us."

Mrs. Chester nodded and ran a finger under Molly's soft chin. "April's over on a blanket by the baseball diamond," she said to me. "Why don't you run on ahead while I talk baby with your folks?"

I walked slowly, but too soon I was standing in front of

April. She was sprawled out on the blanket, coloring book open in front of her and a bag of cheesy crackers spilled out beside her. I knew she saw me—I put a big shadow over the superhero she was coloring—but she didn't look up. Just behind her, one of her brothers was lying flat on his back, sound asleep.

"Hey," I said. I folded my legs and sat crisscross-applesauce beside her.

"Hey," she murmured.

"Is he okay?" I asked, pointing to her brother, whose drool was forming a little puddle beside his head.

"Still trying allergy medicine," she said. "We're allergic to grass!"

I took it as a good sign that she was back to yelling everything. Maybe she forgave me. April sneezed, and I quickly handed her a tissue from the box on the blanket. She smiled and wiped. Then April shifted a little to the side and moved the coloring book so the blank page was in front of me. She plopped a huge plastic bag of crayons between us. I lay beside her and picked up a crayon. "Thanks," I said.

April shrugged. "Scrappy's up! He's—"

"Awesome?" I interrupted. "Yeah, he told me."

April giggled as Scrappy swung at the ball and twisted entirely around, missing it. He did the same thing three more times before finally knocking the ball a few feet in front of him. He ran full force and slid into first, even though no one was even trying to get him out. The other team's players tackled each other to grab the ball. Soon I was giggling, too.

It was a happy day.

Until Becky showed up.

Chapter Nine

"I've got to go," I told April.

I didn't wait for her to answer, but just took off toward Mom and Dad, who were still talking with Mrs. Chester. I glanced back at April, feeling a little guilty about leaving like that, and caught her just in time in a whole-body sneeze. Becky was walking behind April's blanket toward the baseball diamond next to where Scrappy was playing. Her pretty face puckered with disgust when April used a tissue to wipe whatever flew from her nose off the blanket.

My eyes tracked Becky as she sauntered over to the other field. I shuddered—honestly shuddered—when I saw where she was headed. Tom was standing to the side of the diamond, watching a different game. I remembered then: he had an older brother who played Little League. Well, great. Maybe, if I was lucky, he hadn't seen me. Maybe Becky hadn't either.

But then Becky's horrid giggle trickled across the field and both she and Tom turned toward April's blanket. Then Becky jerked her thumb toward me! And they both laughed. I felt my face burn.

"Lucy?" Dad asked as I approached. "Isn't that Becky? Why don't you go say hi?" He waved with big windshield wiper arms to Becky and Tom. I guess Operation Be Happy was back in effect for him and Mom. Becky's mouth fell open and Tom quickly turned his back. Becky gave a pathetic little half wave and collapsed into more giggling, falling into Tom. Now my eyes were burning, too.

"Can we go home now? Please?" I mumbled.

Mrs. Chester squeezed Mom's arm and told her she'd give her a call soon, then headed off toward April's blanket.

"Why, sweetie?" Mom asked after saying goodbye to Mrs. Chester. "Your friends are here. Why don't you go play while we take Molly for a walk?"

I shook my head. Mom's fingers, gentle but firm, grasped my chin and tilted my head toward her. "Oh man," she whispered. "We forgot to put on sunscreen, didn't we? Your face is flaming!"

"Her arms look all right, though," said Dad, poking my still milky white arms, while Mom rooted through her enormous diaper bag for sunscreen. Dad held his hands over my head like a visor, and Mom blew air across my face while her hands searched the bag. Seriously. Now, of all times, Mom and Dad had to pay attention to me. Even though I didn't want to, I glanced back toward Becky and Tom, who were openly staring at me and laughing. I accidentally-on-purpose bumped Molly's stroller. Her arms flew out like the sky was about to fall on her.

Never was I happier to hear her shrieking!

"Lucy!" Dad admonished.

"Sorry," I chirped. "We should go, though. I mean, she sounds hungry or something."

Mom sighed, her smile wobbling for a second, and she gave up searching for sunscreen. "Yeah, it's been a long morning. I'm ready for a nap."

We walked back home, Molly screaming the whole way and Dad still trying to keep the sun off my face.

For the rest of the day, I waited for the phone to ring, for Becky to call and tell me how ridiculous I looked with Mom and Dad and to call me out for sitting with April. I was ready for the call. I was going to scream at her about how she wasn't just pretending not to be my friend; she was going out of her way to be mean. I was going to tell her she didn't have to pretend any more. We weren't friends.

I would say that, unlike her, I wasn't willing to do anything it took to be popular. I wasn't going to be mean to people who were nice to me and be friendly to people who were mean. I was through with her and was going to make my own pack. I mean, friends.

But she never called. And, truth is, I wouldn't have said any of that, even if she had.

"You're really quiet today," Sam said. He sat across from me on top of the monkey bars. I don't know when it happened, but we were spending recess together now, too. Both of us seemed to migrate to the same part of the playground. It was the old section, which just had one set of metal monkey bars and a metal sliding board tucked off in a corner of the playground. Everyone else swarmed on the new bright red playscape, with its tunnels, twisty slide, and rings that you could pedal with your arms to get from one side to the other. Sam and I perched on the monkey bars. The only people nearby were Sheldon and April, who hung out on the slide, and Amanda, who hammered the tetherball by herself.

I looked at Sam. "That's funny, coming from you."

Sam rolled his eyes. I noticed that while he didn't talk much, he said a lot with his face. When he was frustrated, he rolled his eyes. When he was mad, he squeezed his eyes shut and his mouth made a straight white line. When he was happy, his cheeks got a little pink and a dimple popped in his left cheek. When I first came into Ms. Drake's classroom in the morning, he had this little half-smile and his eyes followed me from the door to my seat. I wasn't sure what that meant he was feeling, but I liked when it happened.

Maybe I was spending too much time looking at his face.

Right now his eyes were circles and his cheeks bright red. I guess that's his why-are-you-staring-at-me face. And then he asked, "Why are you staring at me?"

I shrugged, fighting off the blush I knew was creeping onto my cheeks. "Just trying to think of a new bet."

Sam smiled. "Make it a good one. The last one was lame."

Right before lunch, I had bet him that he couldn't go an hour without using his thumbs. Watching him try to eat fish sticks using his pointer and middle finger was hilarious. They crumbled into disgusting, smelly flakes.

"Well, technically, it's your turn for a bet," I said.

Sam bit his lip for a second. "Got it! You have to get from one side of the monkey bars to the other and back without falling."

I jumped off the bars. "No prob." I was a bit of a monkey bar expert, to tell the truth. I whipped across the bars and twisted at the last rung to head back. At the last grab, the skin at the base of my fingers started to sting, but it wasn't too bad. I saw Amanda edging closer from the corner of my eye, probably ready to point and laugh if I fell.

"Your turn," I said as I landed. "But I bet you can't go back and forth twice."

"No prob." And holy moly! Sam whipped from one side to the other in seconds, twisted with this awesome jumpy action and grasped the inside rung with his fingertips. Then he whipped to the end and did it again. Being an absolute show off, he even went an extra run.

"That was amazing!" I yelled. Sheldon and April had stopped going down the slide to watch, April with her mouth hanging open and Sheldon doing a slow clap.

Sam gave me his your-turn look, but I ignored it. No way could I follow up that performance. Instead, I pointed to the grassy stretch beside the monkey bars. "Do a cartwheel!" I dared.

Sam rolled his eyes. "I don't do cartwheels."

Something in the way he said it made it sound like he *could* do something cooler than cartwheels. "All right," I said. "Then show me what you can do."

Sam smiled and looked around. No one seemed to be paying attention to us. And then, he was flipping. Seriously! It was a cartwheel, but his legs were together. From that, without even hesitating, he did a back flip. For real! And then another one. All of this was in about two seconds flat.

Amanda, her arms crossed, snapped, "Bet you can't do it with one hand."

Sam smiled, his cheeks pinker than normal, and did the same routine—cartwheel thingy into two back flips. But with only one hand touching the ground. I clapped so hard my hands felt sunburned.

When he landed, I saw that more kids were watching, even Becky.

Amanda tried not to smile, but the corner of her mouth was twitching. "No hands," she challenged.

He looked so, well, talented. And strong. I noticed that

his arms had muscles that I didn't have. I was pretty sure even sporty guys like Tom and Henry didn't have strong arms like that. From on top of the new playscape, Tom and Henry glared over at us. I fought the urge to stick out my tongue at them.

Sam grinned and did a backflip again. Without any hands!

"Awesome!" I cheered. Everyone clapped and April whistled. This time, Tom and Henry's mouths hung open.

"That was so cool," Amanda whispered as everyone lined up to go back inside after recess.

"Yeah," came Henry's snort. "Hey, Righter, my animal report's on monkeys. Can I interview you?" Henry rushed to the front of the line as Ms. Drake opened the door, bumping Sam on purpose and making him fall onto his knees. Of course almost everyone laughed.

I took a long breath from my nose. I was so angry I probably could've farted a lollipop. I could hear Sam's teeth grind, but he was too busy staring at his sneakers for me to see what his face was saying.

"I thought it was amazing," I whispered when he sat down at his desk in front of me. Sam didn't even turn around. Only the smallest tilt of his head my way let me know that he even heard me. "How did you learn how to do that?"

He shrugged his shoulders.

Tom asked to use the pencil sharpener, which was on the wall beside our row. "Ooo-oo, ah-ah!" he hissed like a monkey as he walked by. I glared at him as hard as I could.

"Ignore him," I whispered to Sam. But this time he didn't act like he heard me at all. He slouched as low as he could in his desk and didn't speak, smile, or move until Ms. Drake dismissed us at the end of the day. And then he wouldn't get up from the desk until everyone—including me—left the room.

I was really beginning to wonder what I had ever seen in Tom.

During gym class the next day, the boys got to play kickball while the girls had to go into another classroom and listen to the nurse talk about all the "exciting changes" about to happen as we "embrace our womanhood." I will never speak of what I learned and refuse to believe it.

So the girls were already lined up for lunch in the cafeteria when the boys entered, sweaty and happy and loud. Tom and Henry made it to the line behind the girls first, and out of loyalty to Sam (and, let's be honest, a general annoyance with boys), I turned on my heel and would not look back.

Hoping for a chance to distract Sam from being called a monkey so much today, I loaded my tray with dare-worthy foods—the plastic-y pink moist stuff the lunch ladies called "turkey ham," creamed corn, and refried beans. (Sidetrack here, but the beans only look gross. They taste divine. I usually gobble them down in three quick spoonfuls when the bell rings and no one's looking.) But when I got to our table, Sam wasn't there.

A few tables away, Becky was holding her stomach, forcing out a laugh that was too loud and stinging to be real. Tom sat back in his chair, his elbows hooked on the sides and his legs spread out straight in front of him. It was like he was taking up as much room as he could; just the opposite of Sam trying to disappear during class. Henry was bragging about something to Becky, his face red and his grin huge.

I stared at my tray, letting the sloshy something's-wrong feeling in my stomach churn.

"Oh no! Really?" April's undeniable screech pulled my attention away from the tray. She and Sheldon were sitting at the table just behind me. I half-turned toward them so they would know I was listening.

"Yeah," Sheldon said. "First, Tom hit Sam right in the you-know-what during kickball. Coach was so steamed, Tom had to sit out the rest of the game. But you could see Tom smiling the whole time. I mean, he looked like a Dimetroden, his smile was so big."

"Wow!" April said politely.

"Forget the dinosaur!" I broke in. "Then what happened?"

Sheldon and April both stared at me. Then, very slowly, Sheldon said, "The Dimetroden isn't a dinosaur. It was warm-blooded and therefore obviously not a dinosaur."

I stared back. "Fine. Not a dinosaur. What happened to Sam?" I hissed.

"Finding out about your monkey boy?" Henry's stupid snorty voice came from just behind me. "Don't worry; he's just *hung up* at the moment." Tom and Becky bellowed from across the room.

"You're such a jerk!" I snapped. But I didn't use the word jerk. I used the word Grandma had used that I'm not supposed to say but find myself thinking a lot recently.

Henry's already red face flared. "Whoops," he muttered and then tipped my tray right onto my lap. How dare he touch my beans! The turkey ham landed with a plop on the floor beside me, but the beans and creamed corn splattered my jeans from my waist to my ankle.

"Ugh!"

"Jerk!" April shouted. But she didn't use the word jerk, either. And she said it a lot louder than I did.

Ms. Drake was at our table in three seconds flat. "You!" she pointed to April. "Principal's office! Now!" April's manner of speaking was pretty effective, I guess. And maybe a little contagious. "You!" Ms. Drake pointed to Henry. "Apologize!"

"Sorry," Henry smirked.

"Not forgiven," I answered.

Ms. Drake rolled her eyes and then jabbed her finger my way. "You! Go to the girls' locker room and see if you can clean yourself up." Her voice dipped a little quieter, which was pointless since the entire cafeteria was staring at us. "If you can't, there's a lost-and-found box with clothes that might fit. Just make sure you don't try on any hats. That's how the Great Lice Infestation of 1994 began."

I ran to the locker room, dripping pieces of mushy corn all the way. I wanted to clean up fast and get back to class where I could hopefully find out what happened to Sam. That swirly sick feeling in my stomach was only growing worse. I didn't even bother trying to clean up my jeans. They were so tight at the waist anyway, taking them off felt like a relief. I dumped out the lost and found box and found a black skirt that, while looking ridiculous with my brown T-shirt, at least wasn't crusted with creamed corn. The waist band was elastic, so it fit better than my jeans did, but it felt like a tube across my thighs and backside. The center seam in front and across the back was so stretched it looked like a gray line down the middle of the skirt. I caught a glimpse of myself in the locker room mirror and realized I looked like a stuffed sausage. But my other option was a pair of pink shorts with purple unicorns. So I stuck with the sausage skirt.

I was shaking so hard and my heart was pattering so fast with worry and anger as I left the locker room. My fingertip hold on my slimy jeans slipped, and I caught them by the leg. All the change I've been carrying around in my pockets for months now (in case I caved to Henry's demands for payment of Tom's lost ring) scattered across the floor. I mean, we're talking about five bucks worth of nickels, dimes, and quarters.

Well, actually, just one quarter. And the big money, of course, slipped right under the boys' locker room door. Darn it! I pressed my ear against the door; the locker room was si-lent. I had passed Coach heading to the cafeteria as I was going to the locker room—he yelled at me not to run (which is a little ironic, if you think about it, given how he usually screams at me to move faster). So I knew there shouldn't be anyone in the locker room. But still. It was the boys' locker room.

I took a deep steadying breath and thought of the quarter. I pushed the door open. The coin had slid just to the edge of the tiled partition that opened up to the locker room. I had to admit, I was surprised that this locker room looked just like ours. I thought it would be bluer. And maybe it would stink more. Not that it smelled great, but it wasn't any worse than the girls' locker room.

"Hmm," I murmured and pocketed my coin.

I was just about to scoot out of there when I heard a sob. It was soft, like whoever it was didn't want anyone to hear, but also desperate.

And I thought I knew who was making that sound.

Biting my lip, I crept forward and peeked past the partition. I gasped.

Hanging from the hooks lining the wall was Sam. He was suspended there by the waistband of his jeans and underwear. His feet were off the floor. He tried to scoot his feet along the wall to boost himself up enough to get off the hook, but I could see it was useless. He was trapped.

Sam's eyes were red and his face slick with tears. I could see the angry red tracks where they had streamed down his cheeks. He looked, well, he looked pathetic.

"Go away, Lucy," he sobbed.

And I wanted to. But I didn't.

I helped my friend.

After that stupid moment of just taking this in, I rushed forward. With my shoulder, I hoisted Sam up enough to get his pants' band off the hook. He slumped forward, and we both sort of fell to the locker room floor. Instantly, his hands shot out and shoved me back. I landed with a thump on my backside.

"Get away, Lucy!" he snapped, tears still pouring out of his swollen eyes.

I stink at listening. I slowly stood up instead of leaving. "Are you okay?" I whispered. "I mean, obviously you're not okay. But are you hurt anywhere?"

Sam ground the palms of his hands into his eyes. His shoulders shook super-fast. "I shouldn't have done that . . . the thing on the bars and then those flips. I'm so stupid. Stupid!"

Now I was shaking my head. "No," I said, stepping toward Sam with my hand outstretched but not actually touching him. "No, that was incredible. They're just jerks, Sam. Jerks!"

"I know," he whispered back. But then he sort of growled and the next words came out as yells. "I know that, Lucy! We both *know that*! But I put myself out there, with like, a big stupid target on my back. For nothing! For nothing. I'm so stupid!"

"Quit that!" I snapped back. "Quit calling my friend stupid. They're stupid. We're going to go to the principal. When we tell him what they did, they'll get their stupid butts expelled and—"

"No!" Sam yelled. He jumped to his feet. His hands were in fists now and they slammed into his sides. "No! We're not telling anyone." His eyes, red and raw, seared into mine. "We're not telling anyone ever, Lucy. Ever!"

"Sam," I said. "Everyone already knows. They were talking about it at lunch."

He turned on his heel and kicked the wall. He whipped back around. "We're. Not. Telling."

"All right," I agreed. "It's your call. Even if it's a stupid decision, it's your decision. I'm sure kicking locker room walls will also take care of our problem."

"We don't have a problem, Lucy. *I* do. Now will you get out of the boys' locker room?"

I stared at him. I know it's selfish. I totally get that I was being a selfish person. But here was my honest worry: Is he not going to be my friend anymore? Will he not do dares with me at lunch or sit at my table? Was I on my own again?

I walked slowly from the locker room, the door slamming shut behind me.

Chapter Ten

"Thank you for choosing to rejoin us today, Lucy," Ms. Drake said as I walked back into the classroom.

I didn't bother responding, just marched across the room to my desk. Sam's seat was empty. Somehow that blank spot in the room seemed to tunnel everyone's whispers straight to me. Tom, Becky, and Henry's lowered voices and stupid giggles were loudest, of course, but I also could hear April, Sheldon, Amanda, and everyone else in our class buzzing like gnats. Sam's name was mentioned a lot.

The minutes ticked by. Still, no Sam. I couldn't stop my eyes from darting between the clock on the wall and the class-room door. Where was he? I shouldn't have left him alone and crying. Should I tell Ms. Drake? Why wasn't she freaking out about missing one of her students in the middle of the day? Sam's seat was in the front row for goodness sake! How could she not see that he was missing?

And then I realized that Sam was easy to overlook, even for our teacher. I mean, I had barely noticed him all year. It wasn't until I had no one else to talk to and was situated just behind him that I even remembered that Sam Righter was in our class.

I thought about what he had said in the locker room, about putting himself out there. He was right: He was only picked on after he did something to bring attention to himself. But why? I squeezed my temples with my hands, trying to massage my memory into conjuring up what I knew about Sam prior to this year. I had nothing. How could I be in the same class as someone for five years (counting kindergarten) and not remember anything about him? I thought about how Sam had sat, slouched in his chair. About how he rarely spoke, never volunteered for anything, hung out alone at the library, couldn't be found at recess. Then I realized: Sam didn't want to be noticed. He wanted to blend into the background. And stupid me had to go and ruin everything.

He was a scapegoat, and I had pushed him to fight back. Now life was a million times worse for him.

"Ms. Drake?" The classroom intercom switched on and the office secretary's scratchy voice echoed through the suddenly quiet classroom. Henry and Tom looked a little pale and sweaty. I crossed my fingers under the desk and hoped that Sam had changed his mind and went to the principal. I hoped, hoped, hoped that Henry and Tom were going to be called to the office and expelled. Or maybe just hung by their underpants for an hour. That'd be fine with me, too.

But instead the secretary said, "Just letting you know that one of your students, Sam Righter, isn't feeling well. He's in the nurse's office now, and his parents are on their way."

Tom and Henry grinned at each other.

"Thank you," Ms. Drake called out. She frowned and glanced at Sam's empty desk. "Has anyone seen Sam since lunch?"

"He wasn't at lunch!" April called. Meeting with the principal apparently didn't do too much to curb her outbursts.

Tom snort laughed.

"Something amusing you, Tom?" asked Ms. Drake, her frown about to touch her neck.

Tom shook his head, smile gone, and said, "I think I saw him hanging around the locker room after gym." Henry cough laughed. And I exploded.

Without even thinking about it, I jumped to my feet, my arms outstretched like I was about to bolt over three rows of desks and attack Tom and Henry.

"Shut up!" I screamed. I mean, *really* screamed. All the notebooks, pencils, and papers on desks between me and the two of them flew into the air around me like a storm cloud. (Okay, that didn't really happen. But I felt like it could've, that's how loud I screamed.) I screamed so loud that it echoed with an enormous ripping sound.

Ms. Drake whipped toward me. Her mouth popped open. Tom and Henry looked at me, mouths hanging open, too. And then, they laughed. Soon the whole classroom was giggling and pointing at me. Well, not really me. They were pointing at my lost-and-found skirt. That ripping sound wasn't an echo. It was the skirt splitting at the seam all the way to the elastic waist when I popped to my feet.

I gasped and grabbed the fabric in my fist, trying to hold it together, but that just made another rip across the backside, showing everyone in the row behind me my polka-dotted underwear. I gasped again and grabbed fistfuls of fabric in front and behind.

Ms. Drake rushed to the front of the room, whipped her

sweater off the back of her chair and wrapped it around my waist. "Go ahead and get back to the locker room. Then come straight back here." Her eyes were fierce.

I spent the rest of the day in a brown T-shirt, the hem crusted with refried beans and creamed corn, and pink unicorn shorts. I slouched down in my desk, wishing I were invisible.

When the bell rang at last and we headed to the bus line, Ms. Drake wrapped her cool fingers around my wrist to hold me in place. "I'll be calling your parents this evening, Lucy. Is there anything you'd like to share with me beforehand?" Her face was surprisingly kind, given that she was about to ruin my life even more. I shook my head.

The smart thing to do would have been to tell Mom immediately after school that Ms. Drake would be calling. I'd tell her that I yelled during class and split my skirt and that I wouldn't do it again. That way, I could go on with my evening, not worrying that every time the phone rang, I'd be doomed. But a small part of me hoped that Ms. Drake might forget to call. And then I'd be telling on myself. Which would be a not-smart thing to do.

I still wasn't sure which part of me I'd listen to when I got to my driveway. Grandma's car was behind Mom's van.

I quietly opened the screen door. Mom and Grandma were at the kitchen table. Mom was crying, her head on her arms, and Grandma was patting her back. Molly was fast asleep in her car seat, placed in the middle of the table between them.

"Does this mean we're done being happy?" I blurted. "Thank goodness."

Grandma and Mom's heads shot up like groundhogs. For a second, they just stared at me in all of my pink unicorn, re-fried bean-crusted ridiculousness. Then they both burst out laughing. Mom held her arms out to me and I practically ran to the other side of the table and into her arms. "Oh, baby," she crooned, her eyes still teary. "What happened to you to-day? What the heck are you wearing?"

I shook my head, burying it into her shoulder. Her shirt was soon wet with my tears.

"Tell us what's going on with you," Grandma ordered.

But just as I was about to figure out how to answer, the phone rang.

Hours later, Mom and Dad sat at one side of the kitchen table and I slumped in a chair on the other side. Grandma, uncharacteristically quiet, rocked Molly in the living room.

"So, you yell at your classmates now?" Dad's voice was grim.

I stared at the tabletop. There was a sticky glob on the tablecloth that sometimes looked like Pennsylvania, sometimes like Connecticut.

"Honey," Mom's voice was sickly sweet. This is how they do things. One of them is mean so the other can be nice. And then they switch, without warning. "We want to understand so maybe we can help you. What made you yell in class today?"

Dad crossed his arms and glared at me. "Ms. Drake said she is pretty sure that lunch tray didn't accidentally spill onto your lap. What did you do to provoke that?"

Now I glared back. Of course they would think *I* did something to provoke it. When really, when it comes down to it, it's *their* fault. If Dad would've just taken me back to the hospital for my diamond ring, none of this would've happened. None of it!

But that's not true, that quiet, annoying voice in my head whispered. Everything started to fall apart behind the ball shed. Or even earlier. When did I first notice that Tom wasn't exactly a nice person? When he would make fun of April at recess? When he would push Sheldon as he walked by in the hall? When he would ignore me if no one was looking?

When did I notice that Becky wasn't really a good friend? Because her offer to "pretend" not to like me wasn't as shocking as it probably should've been. The clues had been there all along.

And, that quiet voice whispered even softer, when did I realize that *I* wasn't a good friend? I laughed as hard as anyone when Tom made fun of April. I made fun of her, too. I just rolled my eyes when he pushed Sheldon. And—honesty alert here—I liked being Becky's *friend* more than I liked Becky. Wasn't I just as guilty of doing anything it took to be popular? If Becky was the one whose kiss was lame, would I be the one who was pretending to be her friend right now? I rubbed at my face, trying to mash my thoughts away. I didn't know the answers to these questions. But I did know one thing: I wasn't willing to do anything it took to be popular. Not anymore.

"Ms. Drake also told us about your skirt splitting," Mom said softly. "That must've been really embarrassing."

I stared at the glob, but nodded a little. It was embarrassing, but nothing compared to what happened to Sam.

"How can we help you?" Dad asked. Uh-oh. Looks like they're switching off to him being nice and Mom being mean. But when I looked up, neither seemed angry any more.

"I don't know," I shrugged.

"Being your age is tough," Dad said. "I get it. I went through it, too. But it will get better. People grow up. They realize how they can hurt others. They change, and it gets better."

"Will it?" I whispered.

"Of course it does, honey," Mom said.

"Then why were you crying today?" I crossed my arms. "If things get easier—if people figure out how to be nice—why is everyone so upset about Molly? It's because she's going to get picked on, isn't it?"

Picked on by jerks like Tom and Henry. Laughed at by jerks like me. Ignored by everyone else, especially those who were just trying not to be noticed themselves, like Sam. Everything—everyone—seemed so bleak.

"You were crying today? Again?" Dad turned on Mom. Her face flushed. I squirmed in my seat. What did I do now?

Grandma to the rescue. She waddled in on her thick, sandaled feet and sat at the table.

"We're trying to keep this a family discussion," Mom said to Grandma, an edge to her voice.

Grandma's voice matched it. "Well, you're doing a crap job of it." She turned toward me, her mouth a firm straight line and her eyes blurry beads behind her smudged-up glasses. "Molly's going to get picked on. You're already getting picked on. Everyone in this world gets picked on at some point—some people more than others, some people less. A few protect themselves by being bullies. Some are able to ignore the bullies and embrace who they are. Those folks are rare. Everyone else struggles."

"Well, that stinks," I muttered.

Grandma's round face wobbled as she nodded. "It does. I suggest you embrace who you are."

"That's a bit easier said than done," Dad said. I didn't think he was talking about me anymore.

Grandma lowered herself into a chair. "What you need is a distraction. You all need a distraction." She turned her beady eyes on her own daughter. "And you need a hobby."

"Molly is only a few months old!" Mom snapped. "I hardly have time to shower between feedings and diaper changes, let alone take up crochet."

Grandma huffed. "No one's talking about crochet. But you need some time to yourself. I have an idea." She turned back to me. "You need to learn how to stick up for yourself without making yourself out to be an idiot."

"Mom!" "Grandma!" Mom and I both shouted at once. Dad laughed.

Grandma continued like we hadn't spoken at all. "I'm signing you up for karate."

"No, thanks," I said.

"I'm not giving you a choice," Grandma replied. "I'll bring Molly along when I take Lucy to lessons. That'll give you two hours a week to yourself, to do whatever. Shower, maybe." Her beady eyes raked up Mom's sweatpants and pajama-top combo and her frizzy ponytail.

Mom flushed. "That'd be nice," she murmured.

"We don't have the money for karate lessons right now," Dad mumbled. He shoved his hands through his hair.

"Lucy's birthday is next month," Grandma said. "Let's consider this her gift from me."

"Do I get any say in this?" I snapped. I had plans for my birthday; it was the one day I figured it'd be all right to break my don't-ask-for-anything vow. Some new shoes, a couple new outfits, maybe some make up. Karate lessons were definitely not on the list.

Grandma got up from the table. "No," she answered. Dad and Mom got up, too.

"Grrr!" I growled.

"Hi-yah!" Dad replied, karate chopping the air with his hand.

My life stinks.

Chapter Eleven

I stormed from the house, whipping open the screen door and getting ready to run to the creek until dinnertime. Maybe even bedtime. But instead I ran full force into April.

"What are you doing here?" I asked.

"I wanted to tell you something! But I heard you get in trouble! So I just waited!"

"Were you listening?"

April nodded. "Karate! I want to take karate, too! Mom says I need an activity!"

"Great," Grandma called out, who also seemed to be an expert at eavesdropping. "I'll take you to class, too. We're going to Miss Betsy's Marital Arts."

"Miss Betsy's?" My confidence-boosting, life-salvaging

karate teacher was named Miss Betsy? "How do you know Miss Betsy?"

Grandma, not moving any closer to the door, shouted, "Remember me telling you I wasn't so nice when I was kid? Betsy was one of those kids I wasn't so nice to. And then she started taking karate. Wouldn't take any crap after that."

"But doesn't that mean that Miss Betsy is . . . old?" I asked.

That got Grandma moving. Her steps thundered toward the door. "What was that, dearie? I couldn't hear you. Must've forgotten my hearing aids, given how much an oldy moldy I am." She rolled her eyes.

"Grandma!" I snapped.

"Lucy!" she snapped back.

"Yay!" April clapped her hands. "Let's start next week!"

"Classes are Wednesdays and Fridays. I'll pick you up at five o'clock," Grandma called as she walked back into the house.

"Grrr!" I growled but no one listened. "Why are you here?" I asked April again.

"Wolves!" she chirped.

"What about wolves?" I asked. Fighting to keep my tone

so she wouldn't see how annoyed I was, I added, "You don't need to shout it. Just tell me. I'll listen until you're done."

April's eyes widened for a second. It was like she didn't know how to speak with someone actively listening. Her mouth opened and closed like a guppy fish. Finally she said, "I wanted to let you know that my mom's sister, Aunt Shelly, works at a wolf sanctuary. She actually lives there, too, like a caretaker. Mom says that's why she's so strange, living by herself with just wolves."

She paused and looked at me. I nodded, and she continued, "If you want to go there sometime, Aunt Shelly said she'd give you and Sam a tour. So you could see real wolves." She grinned. "It's a couple hours' drive from here."

I grinned back. "That's great, April! Thank you!"

"You're welcome!"

"All right!"

"All right!"

"Want to play?" I asked her. "At the creek?"

"Sure!" she said. "We can find frogs!"

Yelling was kind of a fun way of talking.

"Hold on a sec!" I called and ran back inside. I grabbed a travel pack of tissues from the bathroom closet. When I got back to the porch, I handed it to April. "Look, I like hanging out with you. But the nose picking thing—"

"I have allergies!"

"I know. But use tissues, April. Really. Our friendship depends on it."

From the way she smiled at me, I knew her mind had caught on the word "friendship." It made me remember when Sam first called me his friend that time in the library. I smiled back at April, and we ran to the creek.

Sam wasn't in school the next day. I was itching to tell him about April's aunt's wolf sanctuary. Just thinking about it made me momentarily forget the whole splitting-my-skirt-and-yelling-at-everyone episode. Sadly, Tom and Henry did not forget. Neither did Amanda, who laughed hysterically and kept trying to give me fist bumps. (Side note: It took a long time for me to figure out that she was trying to do that and not punch me. I almost peed myself the first time her hand shot out toward me.) Henry made ripping noises as I sat down in my seat. Becky laughed her stupid girly laugh the whole time.

Ms. Drake clapped her hands. "Enough!" She smiled

kindly at me, which, of course, only made everyone laugh harder. "Settle down, everyone."

I spent the rest of the day staring at the back of Sam's empty seat, and sitting alone on the monkey bars at recess and at our table during lunch. Part of me was worried about Sam. Maybe he really was sick? Another part was feeling a little angry that he abandoned me like this. But most of me was thinking about how cool it would be to have a selective hearing super power, so I wouldn't have to listen to everyone around me hissing like flies. At least April walked home with me from the bus.

Sam wasn't in school the next day, either. Or the day after that.

I tried calling his home, but his mom always said that Sam was taking a nap. But there was such a long pause between when she said she'd go get him and when she came back, that I knew she was covering for him. He just didn't want to talk to me.

It was totally unfair! If he wants to be mad at me for seeing him in the locker room, fine. I mean, it was stupid of him, of course. But I could understand being that embarrassed. (After all, I was glad Sam hadn't see the splitting of the sausage skirt incident.) However, he was still my partner for the wolf report and that made up a huge chunk of our grade. Plus, seeing the wolves up close at the sanctuary would be incredible. *Grrr!*

"Loser!" Henry called over to me on his way to the pencil sharpener.

I only had time to gobble down a turkey sandwich and some grapes before Grandma picked me up on Wednesday for my first lesson with Miss Betsy.

"Do I really have to do this?" I whined.

She grinned. "Yup."

"Mom?" I whined harder as Grandma herded me through the door.

"You're going."

Grandma made Molly wave a pudgy little hand goodbye to Mom, who looked way too happy to see her two little sunshines leaving the house.

April was waiting for us on her front porch. Even from the driveway, I could hear clanging, shouting, and a scream or two coming from her house. She seemed thrilled to see us; I guess she was looking forward to kicking and punching things.

"Who's excited?" Grandma asked as she pulled into a parking spot at a little strip mall. A sign across the store in front of us spelled out: Miss Betsy's Martial Arts Studio. Even the sign was lame.

But April chirped, "Me! I'm excited! Excited!"

"Double excited? Wow." I get sarcastic when I'm full of dread. April didn't catch on, though, and just smiled.

The studio smelled like gym class but I got a strange whiff of lilacs, too. I soon figured out why when Miss Betsy herself crossed the room. About a dozen kids, both younger and older than us, were already stretching on the huge, cushioned blue mat that spanned the mirror-walled room. Miss Betsy was decked out in a white karate uniform lined in black, a black belt cinched at her waist. Her lips were painted with pale purple lipstick and her hair matched. Seriously, her short curly hair was purple! That's because she was old enough to have purple hair. I glared at Grandma, who seemed to be doing everything possible not to look at me.

"Good afternoon, Irene." Miss Betsy glared at Grandma. She looked sort of like a purplish walnut. Miss Betsy held her wrists behind her back and bounced softly on the balls of her old feet. I got the feeling she was holding her hands back purposefully. "Which of you is the granddaughter and who is the friend?"

"Granddaughter," I muttered.

"Friend!" April chirped.

Miss Betsy nodded at us. She had small wrinkles around her eyes and lips. "You will address me as ma'am or Miss Betsy, is that understood?"

"Um, yes," I shrugged at the same time April said, "Yes, ma'am!"

Miss Betsy turned her glare on me.

"I mean, yes, ma'am," I said a little louder.

"When you step onto this mat," she jerked a thumb behind her, "you will bow toward the flags. The one on the right, of course, is the American flag. The one on the left is the Korean flag. You are about to learn the tenets of Tae Kwon Do." She looked at us, her glare and wrinkles deepening as we looked back.

Grandma nudged me hard in the shoulder.

"Um, yes, ma'am?" I half-questioned, half-responded.

Miss Betsy nodded. *Phew*, I thought. The more Miss Betsy talked, the less she looked like just another old lady with purple hair and the more she looked like someone who could possibly knock another person's face right off. She pushed back the sleeves of her uniform and I could see her arms weren't soft like the saggy chicken skin on Grandma's arms. They were solid and rippled with muscle. I swallowed hard.

Miss Betsy gave us uniforms to put on and directed us to the bathroom. We had to dodge punching bags and a pile of foam-padded blockers on the way to the little restroom in the back of the studio. April yammered away while we changed. I tried to figure out how I was feeling. Angry at Grandma and my parents, of course. Annoyed with April. Scared of Miss Betsy. And I felt a little, tiny flicker of hope. Maybe I could be awesome at this.

Maybe I already was awesome at this. Maybe when Miss Betsy started training us, she'd see that I was a karate prodigy and I'd go straight to black belt. When Tom and Henry threw volleyballs at my head during gym class, maybe I could do a back flip and kick the balls back into their noses. Maybe I could chop spitballs in half midair. Maybe I could do a demo filled with kicks, chops, and jumps on the blacktop at recess and show everyone my mad skills. (Only, of course, my demo wouldn't end with me hanging from my underpants in the locker room.)

But as soon as class started, my hope faded.

Miss Betsy might be evil.

April and I stood in the very back row, the only white belts in a class of about twelve. Some kids smiled as we walked by, but no one talked. Everyone faced forward, hands held behind their backs.

Miss Betsy stood at the front. Everyone bowed to her, except, of course, April and me. April sort of bobbed forward, though. Then Miss Betsy ordered us to do fifty sit-ups. Fifty! Everyone else in the class did one hundred. They paired up, locking their ankles, and popped up and down one hundred times. It took April and me so long to figure out how to connect our ankles that the rest of the class had to wait for us to finish our lame fifty sit-ups. No one made a big deal of it, though. I noticed they all stood, facing forward. No one rolled their eyes or acted bored. Maybe they were happy for the break?

As soon as we were done, I figured we'd be able to get a drink or something, but Miss Betsy just told us to "pound out" twenty push-ups. The rest of the class did forty. After that, we did twenty jumping jacks. And, thanks to the enormous wall of mirrors, I got to see just how ridiculous I jump jack. It's like I don't have actual control of my arms and legs when both are supposed to work together. My legs were going in as my arms were going out. It was horrible! And the more I watched myself, the more I realized everyone else was watching me, too. The rest of the class, even while doing jumping jacks in perfect unison, was watching me not do jumping jacks but sort of an upright spasm. At least no one laughed. One girl, who had a red belt, sort of smiled at me but not in a mean way. I rolled my eyes at her in a can't-believe-we-have-to-do-this way.

"Do you have a problem, Lucy?" Suddenly Miss Betsy's scary face and muscled arms were right in front of me.

"I stink at jumping jacks," I huffed, stilling jumping.

"You stink at jumping jacks *what*?" Her mouth made a white line like Sam's when he's angry.

"I stink at jumping jacks a lot?"

"Ma'am!" Miss Betsy yelled. "You stink at jumping jacks, *ma'am*."

I stared at her. She glared at me. Eventually, I realized that she wasn't calling me ma'am. I was supposed to call her ma'am.

"Oh, right," I said. "Sorry. Ma'am."

Miss Betsy slowly breathed out through her nose. "You'll

improve with practice, Lucy," she said. "Just do your best today. The next class will be a little easier. Before you know it, you'll fit right in." She moved down the line, nodding at April, whose face was tomato red. Her jumping jacks were fine, but she seemed to have forgotten to breathe while doing them. After the jumping jacks, April bent at the waist and gulped like the only oxygen was close to the floor.

Next we had to line up and practice kicking foam-padded targets. Turns out, all my life I've been kicking wrong. Here I thought kicks were simple. *Wham*, kick. Wrong! Kicks are specific. I learned something called a front snap. There are three parts to it: chamber your leg (which is karate-talk for bend your knee), snap your leg (karate-talk for the actual kick), and re-chamber (bend your leg again). There's also something called a roundhouse kick, where you swing your leg to the side and hit with the top of your foot. That one was really fun. I could do it all day! At least, that's what I thought on kick number three. By kick ten, my leg gained about twenty pounds. By kick fifteen, I was sort of crying.

I looked over at the person-sized foam target I was sharing with April. Her narrow face was screwed tight like someone was twisting her mouth. Her hands were clenched in tight fists.

Bam! Bam! Bam! I stopped trying to kick my thousand-pound leg and watched her go. *Bam!* What was she thinking?

Miss Betsy was behind me. Seriously, that old lady has ninja skills because I didn't hear her coming near me at all. But she stood beside me, watching April kick, kick, kick.

"Don't forget to breathe," she said sternly. "And swivel your hips. It'll put more force in your kicks."

Sure enough, April's next kick actually moved the target to the side a little bit. She grinned, her smile splitting that twisty look. She didn't look like the April I knew when she was standing there with her hands in fists, her cheeks rosy and her face slick with sweat and pride. She looked tough.

"Wow, April," I murmured.

"I know! This is awesome!"

Miss Betsy smiled. "You remind me of me in my first class. Feels good to kick stuff, doesn't it? I'd hate to be whoever you were picturing there."

Who was April picturing? Faces from our class flashed in front of me like I was looking at the yearbook. Of course Tom, Henry, and Becky were jerks to April. But so was Amanda. So were the half-dozen or so people who ignore her entirely. So was I.

And that's when I realized, again, what a selfish jerk I am. Because I never once stopped to think about how much it stinks to be April. Here I am feeling sorry for myself because *people might see that she is my friend.* I am such a jerk.

"You're really good at this," I told April.

Miss Betsy turned toward me. The corners of her mouth twitched like she was trying not to smile. She nodded and kept walking.

At the end of class, I was sweaty. Like shirt-sticking-to-my-chest sweaty. I was thirsty, too. Like lap-up-a-puddle thirsty. (You can't get a drink of water during a karate class "unless you're dying," according to Miss Betsy. After class, I was last in line for the water fountain, where everyone took a thousand gulps.) I was more tired than I've ever been before, including the time Dad and I stayed up until four in the morning making a LEGO city.

Part of me never, ever wanted to see Miss Betsy and her evil institution of pain again. But another part—a bigger part—felt proud. I made it through the class. I just wasn't sure I'd be able to make it through another one.

"I'll see you on Friday," Miss Betsy called out as we left.

By the time we dropped off April, the proud feeling was

even stronger than the tired feeling, which is really something.

"You did well," Grandma said to me over the yells, crying,
and laughter pouring out from April's open door as she went
inside her house.

Friday's class was more of the same. Sit-ups, push-ups, kicks,
and punches. Only my muscles were sore from Wednesday, so
my leg turned into a thousand-pound weight right away. But I
made it through the class. And Miss Betsy gave me a high-five
at the end.

"So," Grandma said after dropping off April. "You ready
to admit I was right?"

I shrugged. I wasn't ready to say she was right when I
wasn't even sure why I liked the class. We did nothing but
work ourselves sweaty. I scrunched back in my seat and
thought about it. I guess what I liked more than anything was
that even when April and I took twice as long to do each drill,
no one in the class laughed at us. An older boy told me how
to twist my foot to hit the top of it against the punching bag
when we were doing roundhouse kicks and he didn't make
me feel stupid at all. At the end of class, everyone shook my

hand like I was adult. No one whispered, rolled her eyes, or ignored me when I needed help.

I wanted to be around people like that. I wanted to be a person like that.

"Stop the car!" I screamed to Grandma. She slammed on the brakes. The car behind us screeched to a stop and the driver must've pushed his whole body into the horn, it was so loud.

"What is it? What's wrong?" Grandma screamed.

"That's my friend Sam's house!" And Sam was outside, riding his bike around on his long driveway. So much for being sick!

"You realize I almost killed us, right?" Grandma asked through her teeth. The guy behind us swerved around her car. Grandma shook her fist at him when he made a rude gesture toward us.

"Sorry about that," I said. "Thanks for stopping, though. I really need to talk to him. Can I get out of the car?" But I didn't wait for Grandma's answer. Already I was out of my seat and dashing toward Sam.

He looked up at me for a second and cocked his head to the side like he was confused. I guess having some girl from school stop traffic and dart toward you in a karate uniform is a little startling. I was only a couple feet away from him when he dropped his bike and ran into the house.

"Sam!" I shouted. "You know I totally see you, right? What are you doing?" I ran to the front screen door. I wanted to just throw it open and chase after him, but I knew my mom would never let up on the rudeness lecture if I barged into someone's house. So I took a cue from the angry driver guy and laid on the doorbell.

A confused-looking woman came to the door. Her head whipped from the stairs to me and back a couple times. "Sam?" she called up the stairs just as Grandma huffed to the front door.

"Lucy!" Grandma snapped at me.

Sam's mom and Grandma exchanged a look that I was quite familiar with seeing. It usually came just before an adult sighed and said, "Kids!"

Then Sam's mom smiled, but in a small, sad way. She looked a lot like Sam when she did that. They both have smiles that seem to stop a little too soon. "So, you're the famous Lucy? Sam never stops talking about you."

I didn't know how to answer that, so I just jabbed a thumb toward Grandma. "This is Grandma. Listen, Mrs. Righter, I really, really need to talk to Sam. Really."

Mrs. Righter glanced back up the stairs. "It seems Sam has had a sudden relapse of his mystery illness." She opened the screen door to us. "Come inside. I'll see if I can get him to come down."

I stayed in the foyer, staring up the steps and straining my ears to hear what Sam and his mom were saying, but Grandma wandered into the living room. She let out a low whistle. "You didn't tell me your friend was such an athlete."

The mantle over the living room fireplace was crowded with trophies, most with a big number one on them. Hanging over the mantle were framed pictures of Sam, but all black and white action shots of him doing gymnastics—hoisting himself up and swinging his legs over a pommel horse, hanging by his hands on rings, mid-flip on a high bar.

"I didn't know," I whispered.

Grandma shook her head and whistled again. "Someone doesn't get this good without a lot of practice. You thought your karate lesson was tough? Imagine how much work it took to get in this type of shape."

She was right. Sam had to be practicing all the time to get this good. But he never once talked to me about it.

Just then Sam walked into the room. Or rather, his mom

pushed him in and stood just behind him so he couldn't back out.

"What are you doing here?" he snapped.

"Why didn't you tell me you were this awesome at gymnastics?" I asked back in the same angry voice.

"What's it to you?"

Sam's mom said something in his ear. It sounded like a whisper yell. I caught the words "incredibly rude." Then she straightened up and asked Grandma if she wanted a cup of coffee.

Grandma shifted Molly to her shoulder and squeezed my shoulder. "Sounds great," she said, even though I know she hates coffee. She drinks about a dozen diet colas a day, but says coffee tastes like spit mixed with dirt.

Before they even left the room, I crossed my arms and said, "I thought we were friends."

Sam shrugged.

I stomped my foot. (Mom says I need to work on disguising my frustration. But I think frustration should be obvious.)

Sam looked at his sneakers. "I started gymnastics when I was five, okay? It isn't really a secret. Don't you remember second grade?"

"Parts of it," I mumbled. I got a twisty feeling in my knees. I know a lot of people feel nervous in their stomachs, but for me it's my knees. It feels like someone's twisting and pushing on them at the same time and at any moment they might refuse to hold me upright. "Second grade was two years ago."

Sam gave a small smile. "Show and share? First week of school? I brought this in." He walked over to the mantle and pointed at one of the larger trophies. "Amanda said, 'I thought only girls could be in gymnastics.' Tom and Henry laughed right in front of the Miss Granger. She told them to be quiet—"

"But in an I-think-it's-funny-too way," I remembered. "And then everyone laughed."

Sam nodded and swallowed hard. His smile shook and then left his face. "They kept drawing pictures of me in a leotard and putting them in my backpack. They followed me around the playground asking me to do cartwheels."

He sighed and shrugged. "Mom wouldn't let me quit gymnastics. I was so mad at her about it at first, but the truth is, I really like it." His chin jerked up and he looked at me like he thought I might laugh. "And I'm good at it."

"I can tell. These pictures—you look amazing," I said.

Sam smiled again, a little stronger this time. "I have practice every morning before school and again after school. You could come by class sometime if you want."

I smiled back. "Sure, I'd like that," I said. "And maybe you could come to karate. I take karate now."

Sam laughed and pointed at my uniform. "I figured those weren't PJs."

"Are you coming to school on Monday?"

Sam shrugged. "Dad says I can't keep pretending to get sick every day, but I'm not pretending. Thinking about going back there, seeing them after what they did, it makes me want to throw up."

"I know what you mean." I told Sam about the sausage skirt splitting in class. But somehow, when he laughed as I told him about my ripping skirt, it made me laugh, too. "Want to meet outside the gym and walk to class together?"

"Two losers joining forces?" he laughed.

"Yeah," I said, liking the idea. "We'll be our own pack."

"Pack of scapegoats," Sam added.

"More like pack of dorks, but whatever," I said. And then I told him about April's Aunt Shelley and her wolf sanctuary.

Almost like they were listening in, Grandma and Mrs. Righter came back into the living room just when I finished.

"I'll take you guys there this weekend, if you want," Mrs. Righter said. "It's the only time Sam doesn't have a tournament for the next couple weeks." All right, they were definitely listening in.

As we walked back to her car, Grandma put her heavy hand on my shoulder again. "I'm proud of you, toots."

Chapter Twelve

The wolf sanctuary was about two hours away, according to Mrs. Righter's GPS.

For the first hour, Sam and I talked nonstop, mainly about gymnastics and karate. Since Sam doesn't have any brothers and sisters, he asked a lot of questions about Molly.

"Maybe you should get a little brother or sister?" I suggested, but Sam said he didn't think his mom and dad were up to it.

Mrs. Righter didn't ask any questions or interrupt, but I could see from the way her eyes kept catching ours in the rearview mirror that she was listening to us.

Soon we turned off the highway and headed down a tree-lined road. After a half-hour more, the road stopped being paved and the SUV lurched over rocks and dirt. The only thing I could see out the window was forest. Every few miles, a small wooden sign appeared, printed with ABLE WOLF SANCTUARY AHEAD.

Our talking sort of trickled away as the road narrowed more and more. Mrs. Righter's mouth turned into a straight white line, just like Sam's. Her eyes darted from the GPS to the woods around us. It occurred to me that wolves might not be her favorite animal.

"You know, wolf attacks are super rare," I said a little too loudly.

"The last one was in 2010, when a woman in Alaska was found half-eaten and there were wolf tracks were all around her," said Sam, barely looking up from one of The Goblin's wolf books. I poked him with my elbow. "What?" he whispered.

I rolled my eyes. "But, usually, they're super scared of people."

"Yeah," agreed Sam, looking back at his book. "Most of the time they only bite and mutilate, not kill. It's like a warning, I guess. The only other fatal attack in the last decade was at a Russian zoo, when two eight year olds got too close to the wolves. Seems like they only really go after kids and women."

"Sam!" I hissed.

I noticed that Mrs. Righter's eyes got super wide and she tapped the brakes.

I spied a huge ten-foot-tall metal fence behind the curve of the road. I knew from checking out details about the sanctuary online that the fence also went several feet into the ground. Wolves are good diggers as well as jumpers.

"We're here!" I cheered as soon as I saw the fence gate. I popped out of the car before it was in park, just in case Mrs. Righter decided to turn around. A small speaker was by the gate. I pressed the button and after the ding announced, "Lucy Williams, Sam Righter, and Mrs. Righter, here to see April Chester's Aunt Shelley. Niner-niner. Over and out."

Sam sighed through his nose. "You are such a dork," he said. He pushed me with his shoulder so I knew he didn't mean it in a mean way.

The speaker crackled: "I'll be right there. Hang tight." The voice was growly and harsh, not at all like April's chirping.

While we waited, I stared through the fence to try and spot a wolf pack. But all I saw was a dirt path winding through sparse woods. Farther back I could make out more fences. We had read that packs will defend their territory from other packs, and I saw online that Able Wolf Sanctuary separated its packs with fences. I strained my ears to hear a wolf howl or a bark or something. But aside from a crow's squawking, it was silent. A little too silent, if you ask me. Mrs. Righter was clutching her car keys with white knuckles and eyeing her car. If Aunt Shelley didn't get here soon, we'd be back on the road.

Luckily, a dirty golf cart lurched down the path just then and the person I guessed to be April's Axunt Shelley clamored out.

I was expecting her to be strange, based on what April had said about her. But I was thinking she'd be odd like April is odd. But Aunt Shelley was pretty much April's complete opposite. Aunt Shelley was huge, and not in a likes-her-Snickers-bars sort of way. She was massive like a football player, with wide shoulders and a thick tanned neck. She wore khaki shorts, and her legs also were brown and bulky with muscles. She wore a dirt-smudged hat with ABLE WOLF SANCTUARY printed on it, and her hair was pulled back in a knot at the base of her neck. Strands frayed out from the knot and lay damply plastered to her neck. Her eyes were a dark squinty brown and her mouth a slash across her freckled face. She had the sort of tan that always makes Mom, who is a bit obsessive with the sunscreen, shake her head. She sort of looked like she was made of leather. I thought of scrawny April with her frizzy hair, pale skinny body, and sing-songy voice and wondered if Aunt Shelley had been adopted.

All three of us—Mrs. Righter, Sam, and I—stepped back as the gate was pulled open.

"What are you waiting for?" Aunt Shelley asked. "Come on in. None of the big bad wolves will get you." Her voice was gruff, but when she smiled, I saw how she could be April's aunt. They both have smiles that split their faces.

Sam and I dashed through the gate and climbed onto the back seat of the golf cart. Mrs. Righter paused for a second but finally followed us.

Aunt Shelley locked the gate, yanked on it twice to be sure (or to further freak out Sam's mom, I'm not sure which), and climbed back behind the wheel of the golf cart.

"So," she said, "you want to learn about wolves?"

"It's for a school report," Sam said. Her eyes got even squintier. "But we also really like them a lot," he added.

"Yeah," I said. "They're awesome." She didn't say anything. "Really awesome."

She turned the key in the ignition. Mrs. Righter's hand shot out and grabbed Aunt Shelley's forearm. "So, um, April's Aunt Shelley. Can you tell us a little bit about the sanctuary before we go farther in? Like, um, how many wolves do you have here? And how strong are the fences? Have you tested the wolves for rabies? That sort of thing."

Aunt Shelley sat back in her seat. "Owners will give you all the details," she said. I got the feeling she didn't like speaking too much. She glanced over at Mrs. Righter's wide eyes and seemed to work up a few words. "Able Sanctuary has ten wolves. They're separated into four packs. Or at least, with any luck, they will be by the end of today. Two of the wolves are going to be paired to see if they get along."

"Can we watch that?" I asked.

Aunt Shelley shrugged. "Depends."

"On what?" Sam asked.

She sighed again, long and slow like just living was work. "How it goes," she finally answered.

I imagined April visiting her and had to think April probably loved it. Here was someone who would let her talk as much as she wanted.

"Like I said, the owners will give you the rundown on the

facts about the place," Aunt Shelley said as she shifted into drive and punched the gas. Sam and I grabbed onto the seat in front of us to keep from getting whipped out of the open sides.

"Aunt Shelley?" I asked.

"What?" she answered.

I had meant to ask her what we were supposed to call her, but since she answered to Aunt Shelley pretty quickly, I just muttered "nothing" and held on tight.

We drove past a bunch of fenced-off acres along the dirt road to a building. It was shaped in a circle, with windows on all sides, like buildings people thought everyone would have by the year 2000 way back in the '80s or something. Aunt Shelley pulled into a parking spot between another golf cart and a faded red pick-up truck. Outside the building was a rack of pamphlets with the name of the sanctuary printed across the top and a picture of a gray wolf howling.

Almost the same time I spotted the picture, I heard a howl. In all the books we read, authors were always going on and on about howls—how the first time they heard one it was something they'd never forget; how it chilled them to the bone; and how within seconds the whole air was overtaken with howls as other wolves joined in. Some said it was the happiest noise they ever heard; others said it was like hearing something from another world. I couldn't imagine how impressive it could be. I mean, our neighbor has a dog he keeps fenced in his back yard and the mutt howls all day long. It isn't pretty. It's annoying. Super annoying.

But when I heard this howl, I think I finally understood what the authors meant. This wasn't a sound from a backyard dog. It was much, much different. And it wasn't at all happy. It was sad and long and made gooseflesh pimple across my arms. Aunt Shelley stopped mid-stride and cocked her head to the side while she listened.

"Hang on, Sascha," she murmured. "Almost time."

When the howl finally ended, the silence seemed loud, if that's even possible. Not a single chirping bird or rustle of wind or any usual outside noise. Just silence.

"Aren't other wolves supposed to join in when one howls?" Sam asked.

Aunt Shelley, her voice much softer than before, said, "Not when the wolf is mourning." She picked up her step and swung open the door to the center. "Then they just listen." The heavy door almost closed on Mrs. Righter, who I could tell wasn't used to people not holding doors for her, but Aunt Shelley never slowed or noticed.

The sanctuary owners—Marcia and Adam Able—were much more talkative than Aunt Shelley. We could hear them talking to each other from the moment we walked in, Marcia in high-pitched happy laughs and Adam in endless speech. Marcia laughed with her head thrown back, her short black hair shining in the fluorescent lighting. Adam's pale bald head shone nearly as much. Both of them wore hunter green polo shirts with the outline of the howling wolf I saw on the pamphlet over their breast pocket. Marcia was strong, but not in a wide way like Aunt Shelley. Marcia's muscles were long and lean, like a braided rope lay under her brown skin. Adam was tall and strong, but I didn't notice his muscled arms right away because of the way his stomach pushed against his shirt. He had a soft blonde mustache across his upper lip. It twitched whenever Marcia laughed, which was pretty much always.

Aunt Shelley cleared her throat super loudly.

"Oh!" Marcia said brightly. "We have guests!"

They approached the two of us, hands outstretched for

half-hug, half-handshake moves. They smelled a bit like wet dogs once we were up close. At first Marcia kept calling me Shelley's "little niece" until Sam corrected her and said I was her little niece's friend. But then when Sam called Shelley "Aunt Shelley," I could see Marcia was entirely confused. She kept glancing over at Sam like she was trying to figure out if *he* was Shelley's "little niece."

Adam just went on blabbing. He told us that the sanctuary opened about ten years ago. He said he used to live in the suburbs and his neighbor's dog kept jumping his fence and terrorizing the birds at Adam's birdfeeder—as well as snagging anything he ever brought to the back porch to put on the grill.

"Turns out," Adam said, "it wasn't a dog at all. It was a wolf-dog. And a real bad neighbor." Moustache twitch, moustache twitch.

"A wh—?" Sam started to ask, but Adam was a step ahead with the answer.

"A wolf-dog is a half-wolf, half-dog. These animals can't make it in a domestic situation, you know, one with your mom and dad. They've got too much wild in them." His moustache twitched, and I braced myself for another bad joke. This time Adam elbowed Marcia to give her the heads up one was coming. "Guess that's why I like them so much. I'm a regular wild guy myself." Twitch, twitch.

"Anyway, our neighbor got evicted from his apartment and somehow forgot his dog. About the same time, my folks passed and left me this land. I adopted the dog and brought him here to live like he should. Soon requests came pouring in for more help for wolves and wolf-dogs. I met Marcia, and we decided we were *able* to make a difference. Able Sanctuary. Get it?" He looked as us eagerly. We nodded. I tried hard to roll my eyes only in my mind.

"So, now we house about ten wolves. We try our best to keep their lives as wild and free as possible while also keeping them safe," he said.

"If you don't mind me asking," Mrs. Righter asked, "how do you afford that? I can't imagine the costs involved."

Marcia's smile faltered a little. "We manage," she said, "but it's tough. We mostly operate on donations."

"These animals, they get expensive. They really 'wolf down' the resources! Get it?" Adam said. Twitch, twitch.

I saw Mrs. Righter grab a pamphlet titled ADOPT A WOLF from a rack hanging on the wall. She slipped it into her purse.

Marcia and Adam gave us a quick tour of the center. One

of the rounded walls featured two huge maps of the United States. In one, an orange blob covered most of the map like a massive Sunny-D spill. This showed where wolves once lived. The other had small little splotches along the top of Minnesota, Idaho, Michigan, Montana, Wisconsin, and Wyoming. In the southwest, New Mexico and Arizona had tiny drops of orange also. All of Alaska was covered. This was where wolves now lived.

"Once there were two million wolves in the wild. Now, there are less than sixty thousand left in the whole world," Adam said as we stared at the map.

"What happened?" I asked.

"What happened? Didn't you ever hear of the Big Bad Wolf?" Adam's moustache was startlingly still. "That's what happened. People were sure the wolves were out to get them, out to eat their cattle, kill their babies, decimate the deer population. People killed wolves to the brink of extinction. The government held bounty hunts where so-called hunters got money for turning in just the ears of wolves they killed. Only a few places are left where you can hear wolves and see them roam without fences and safety signs."

"It was because the wolves wanted the same things as humans," Marcia said. I knew what she meant. They wanted to live with their families. They wanted to hunt and to eat. They wanted to have young and grow old. They wanted to continue doing these things in the same places where humans wanted to live, eat, have babies, and grow old. And, worst of all, just like humans, they would fight to protect what they thought was theirs.

"But they were different than humans, too," I said.

"I can relate," Sam muttered.

"What do you say we go see some of the wolves?" Aunt Shelley said, separating the thick silence that seemed to cover us all after Sam spoke.

Chapter Thirteen

Another howl erupted as we left the building, but this one was different. It was high-pitched and somewhat happy. I know, I'm doing that thing scientists and teachers who grade papers hate where people try to give animals human emotions. But I swear, the howl was happy sounding. And a few seconds later, a bunch of other happy yips and howls joined in. Aunt Shelley didn't say anything about it, but she had a huge smile on her face.

We loaded back into the golf cart and headed toward one of the enclosures.

"No touching the animals. No trying to put your fingers through the fence. No standing too close to the fence. Pretty much, just watch from a distance," Aunt Shelley warned as she yanked the cart into park. "Remember, they're wild animals."

"Right," I nodded. Sam put up two fingers in the Boy Scout pledge.

Aunt Shelley smiled as she tossed us two sets of binoculars from the back of the golf cart. A third set hung from a strap on her neck. She raised them up to her eyes and scanned the enclosure. "There!" she pointed.

A few yards out was a giant rock boulder. Under it was a wolf-shaped lump. Once I put on my binoculars, I could see it was a wolf with gray fur and a huge bushy tail. Bouncing around her were two pups, one black and the other splotchy brown. They jumped at each other, going down on their front legs with tails high in the air, then ramming into the adult wolf. She rolled onto her side but didn't move away from the battling pups.

"Aww!" Mrs. Righter said a second after Sam passed his binoculars to his mom.

"How old are the pups?" Sam asked.

Aunt Shelley shrugged. "The people who dropped 'em off said about three months. They wanted wolf-dogs, until they realized how much more wolf they are than dog. Said the pups tore up the carpet in the living room, shredded the couch, and bit the baby."

The two pups rolled over each other, sending up a little dust cloud. One yipped, scooted to his legs, and dashed toward us. The other followed. The gray wolf rolled back onto her legs and watched.

"They were going to be put down at the shelter," Aunt Shelley said, "until Adam took them in. Had to drive across three states to get them."

"Put down?" I asked.

"It means killed," Sam said.

Aunt Shelley nodded. "Wolf-dogs are always killed at shelters. They don't have a chance. And we probably wouldn't have been able to take them if they weren't pups."

The gray wolf—named Luna—was also a wolf-dog. Aunt Shelley told us about half of the sanctuary's population were actually wolf-dogs and not full wolves. She said a few years earlier, Luna's owners drove to the sanctuary and begged Adam and Marcia to take her. She had attacked the neighbor's dog and had to go. If the sanctuary wouldn't take her, she'd be killed.

"Luna fit in right away and joined a pack with Antonia and Winter. They're two of our oldest wolves. *Were* two of our oldest." Her voice caught on "were."

"They passed away?" Mrs. Righter asked softly.

"Yeah," Aunt Shelley grunted. "Winter got sick. Cancer. Died about six months ago. Antonia stopped eating. Tried everything to get her to bounce back. Even Luna would drop food by her muzzle. Nothing worked. Died four months later."

"That's so sad," I said.

Aunt Shelley shrugged. "Animals die. People die. That's the way it works." But the way she crossed her arms like she was holding herself together made me think it wasn't the way Aunt Shelley wanted it to work. "Anyway, we thought Luna would be next. Stopped eating. Stopped playing. Just laid around. Then we got these pups. Took a chance Luna would be maternal. And she is."

By now, Luna was up and trotting toward the pups. I guess they were getting too close to us for her liking. She circled around them and then took off running. The pups chased her, yipping and bouncing like it was the best game ever.

"That's the thing about wolves," Aunt Shelley added. "No matter how much they're messed up from people or other wolves, they always take care of pups. No wolf I've ever met has rejected one."

"What if there is something wrong with a pup?" I whispered.

"What could be wrong with a pup?" Aunt Shelley asked, then turned and went back to the cart. Sam bumped his shoulder gently into mine as he turned, and I knew he did it purpose.

The sad howl we had heard earlier rang out again. Once again, no other wolves joined in. Aunt Shelley stopped walking and listened.

"Let's go meet Sascha," she said.

We wound around more dirt paths to another fenced-in enclosure. Marcia and Adam were already there, holding walkie-talkies to their mouths and staring at the reddish brown wolf pacing a few yards in from the fence.

"Sascha," Aunt Shelley said as if she were introducing us. At the sound of her name, the wolf stopped pacing for a moment and stared at us. Her head tilted upward slightly and her tail rose a little, too.

"She's striking her alpha pose," Aunt Shelley murmured. Another wide smile tugged her leathery cheeks.

"You like this wolf," I said.

Aunt Shelley nodded. "I do."

Marcia moved a little closer. "Shelley's one of the few humans Sascha seems to trust. She came here a few months ago, too mean for the owner's new wife and too skinny to be healthy. She hasn't felt a heck of a lot of love in her life."

"How old is she?" asked Sam, walking a bit closer to the enclosure as Sascha circled slowly toward us. Mrs. Righter grabbed the back of Sam's T-shirt and pulled him back a few inches.

"She's about two years old," Marcia said. "Now that she's closer, check out that bald patch around her neck." I nodded as I glimpsed the bare, raw looking skin around her furry neck. "She was chained up, barely given enough length to stand, for most of the day."

"Except when she figured out how to dig up the spike holding her," Adam said. "Then she'd rip through the neighborhood with the chain dangling behind her, terrorizing lap dogs and demolishing trash cans."

Marcia didn't smile. She bit her lip hard and shook her head. "Despite getting beat every time her owners caught her, despite being trapped and starved as punishment all over again, she misses them."

Adam put a hand on Marcia's shoulder. It was obvious they both really loved this wolf. "And despite her loneliness, Sascha has refused to join any of our packs."

"What do you mean *refused*?" I asked. Sascha, almost like she understood me, growled softly with teeth bared as I stepped closer to the fence.

"I guess she's got trust issues," Marcia laughed. "She attacks any wolf that we've tried to get her to bond with. She's lonely without a pack, but not willing to trust the other animals, either. Especially since the other packs already have alphas—or leaders—and Sascha seems to think of herself as top dog. We try to let the animals react naturally, solve issues the way they would in the wild. But we also have a responsibility to keep them safe. We couldn't let her keep on attacking and being attacked. It was getting dangerous."

"Dangerous?" I asked.

Marcia opened her mouth to answer, but Aunt Shelley beat her to it. "A wolf without a pack, it gets odd acting."

"Sort of like people who live all by themselves," I said. And then I realized that Aunt Shelley lives all by herself. And she was sort of odd, too. My face flamed, and Sam stared at his sneakers. Luckily, Aunt Shelley hadn't picked up on what I had said.

Marcia smiled into the distance. "Exactly."

Adam stepped aside to talk on his radio to another sanctuary worker. A few minutes later, he crunched across the dirt path toward us. He seemed like the kind of person who manages to make a lot of noise doing something other people can do soundlessly. He clapped his hands together and bounced on the balls of his feet. "Hank's bringing Ralph over now. You kids are in for a treat. Or a disaster. One or the other."

"Oh, Adam!" Marcia laughed again, but it sounded strained. Hank, she then told us, was another sanctuary volunteer. Ralph was a new resident.

"Ralph?" I asked.

Marcia's teeth squeaked as she ground them together. "Some workers here believe we've gotten a bit too flowery in our naming of the animals."

Adam turned slightly from Marcia. "We have Luna, Sascha, Balthasar, Sebastian, Cathness, Juno, and Arturo. And then *someone* goes ahead and names those pups Timon and Alcibiades."

"I was an English major, okay!" Marcia turned on Adam with a shriek. Mrs. Righter pulled both Sam and I back by the shoulders. "Those names are *noble*. They have meaning."

"So does Ralph," Aunt Shelley said.

"My dad says ralph instead of puke." Darn it. I did the speaking-out-loud thing again.

Marcia, Adam, and Aunt Shelley stared at me for a moment.

"Is that Hank?" asked Mrs. Righter, her grip not at all loosening on my shoulder. A man drove the beat-up looking red pickup truck we had seen earlier at the center building. A huge dog crate was in the truck bed.

"Kids, into the golf cart, please," motioned Adam, not paying any attention at all when Sam and I grumbled. Mrs. Righter all but pushed us into the cart.

"I seriously doubt being in this golf cart will save us if Ralph goes crazy," Sam pointed out. "I mean, it doesn't even have doors."

It felt a bit refreshing to have someone else state the obvious for a change.

Hank jumped out of the truck, spilling splotches of coffee across his already dirty sanctuary T-shirt. "We're here! We're here! Didn't want to get in the cage, but he did! Now we're here!"

This guy I could totally picture being April's relative. He gulped down some more coffee, then went to the back of the truck. A short bark came from the cage, and I glimpsed dark, almost black fur. Sascha stopped pacing and stared, her tail high and the fur standing almost straight up around her face.

"So, what's Ralph's story?" Sam called out.

I thought everyone would ignore us, but Aunt Shelley came right over. She was as bouncy as Hank, and I guessed some of his energy was more nerves than caffeine. Aunt Shelley told us Ralph had gotten to the sanctuary less than a month earlier. He got loose on a farm where they were breeding wolf-dogs. "Only we think they were more wolf than dog," she said.

Ralph, who was about a year old, was one of the ones the farmers were keeping to breed. Like almost all the animals on the farm, Ralph had been really sick, practically starved and chained up.

"He's got the same bald ring around his neck, only Ralph's collar had never been changed since he was a pup. Our vets had to surgically remove it," Aunt Shelley said.

By now Hank had bounced over toward us. He stood really close to Aunt Shelley, but she kept backing away. Hank didn't seem to notice, just moved closer to her again. Eventually, Aunt Shelley was trapped against the cart.

"Poor Ralph was caught by animal control," Hank said.

"Animal control?" I asked.

"Folks who catch animals and take them to shelters,"

Aunt Shelley said. "Except wolves. They're euthanized."

"That's horrible!" said Mrs. Righter, who covered her mouth with her hand.

"Hey, you're starting to like wolves!" I cheered.

"I wouldn't go that far," she blurted. "No offense," she nodded toward Hank and Aunt Shelley, "but I certainly don't like the idea of systemically killing them."

"Neither do the animal control workers," Aunt Shelley said. "Not all of them, anyway. One gave Adam the heads up that they had collected the animals from the wolf-dog breeding mill. He headed over right away."

"Ralph was at the end of the line," Hank said. "I mean, for real. All these cages were lined up in two rows. The animal control workers held Ralph in a cage at the end. These animal control folks were putting them down, one by one."

"Ralph had to watch every other member of his family be killed," Aunt Shelley said, her chin shaking a little.

"Adam got there in time to save Ralph. Loaded him up and brought him here. Wouldn't talk about what he saw for days," Hank said.

By now, Adam and Marcia had lowered Ralph's cage to the ground. The huge wolf whimpered as they shifted him. As he turned in circles within the enclosure, I saw the angry red slash of skin where his collar had been. I could see his hip bones, too, and indents where his ribs were. I wiped a tear from my cheeks. When I glanced at Sam, I saw his eyes were wet, too.

"Now, listen," Aunt Shelley whispered. "If Adam and Marcia remember you're here, I'm going to have to take you back to the building and miss this. I *don't* want to miss this. So pretend to be invisible."

Good thing we've got a lot of practice at that lately.

Mrs. Righter, Sam, and I barely breathed as Hank unlocked the enclosure around Sascha's territory. The female wolf dashed backward, scrambled to the top of a boulder about a half-acre away, and kept watch as Aunt Shelley opened the gate. Marcia stood by the gate, her hand on her hip, hovering over a tranquilizer gun. Hank and Adam lifted Ralph's cage—with him still in it—to the opening. Adam crooned nonstop to Ralph: "It's going to be okay, buddy. It's going to be just fine."

Hank counted to three and then flipped open the latches on the cage. Aunt Shelley, Adam, and Hank backed out of the enclosure and Hank quickly locked the gate shut.

Sascha stood guard, not moving so much as her ears as

she watched the cage. Ralph didn't move, either.

We all stayed still, silent and barely able to breathe, for what felt like an hour. Really, it might've been fifteen minutes. Slowly, Ralph's front paw stepped out of the cage. Then his second paw touched the dirt. Sascha stayed put, but I noticed her ears flicked around like they were dials on a radio tuning in to a particular station.

So very slowly, Ralph rose and came out of the cage. He stood, his legs quivering, right inside the enclosure. His huge head twisted over toward us. His eyes were the same grayish blue as Molly's. I gasped and the noise seemed to push his head toward Sascha. He made a soft yipping sound and moved toward the bigger reddish wolf.

Sascha leapt from the boulder, her body moving like water as she rushed toward Ralph. Marcia let out a shaky breath and her hand drifted toward her hip again.

"Give 'em a minute," Aunt Shelley murmured.

Sascha circled Ralph, making grunting sounds as she did. Ralph stayed perfectly still, barely moving. Suddenly, Sascha rushed the black wolf. He lowered onto his front paws, his bony rump in the air, his ears flat against his head, and his tongue lolling out of his mouth. Sascha, tail high, stood over him. Her tail swished once, and Ralph's tail sent up clouds of dust as he wagged it slowly across the dirt.

Sascha darted forward and then turned and bounced a foot or two away. Then she turned back and rushed Ralph again. Ralph scooted forward, tail still slowly moving like a pendulum, and then rose to stand. Sascha, her muzzle wide open and tongue rolled out, yipped again and darted away. Ralph followed her this time.

Like a popped balloon, everyone's chests seemed to deflate in unison.

"It worked!" Hank whooped.

"Yes!" Aunt Shelley jumped on the balls of her feet and clapped like a little girl.

Marcia brushed tears from her cheeks and wrapped her arms around Adam, who twirled her around.

"You've just witnessed a new pack being made," Adam called over to us, like he suddenly remembered we were there. "Two animals everyone gave up on found a place with each other."

Somehow a whole day had passed, and as we stood there, listening to the sanctuary workers cheer, the sun began to sink behind the trees.

Sascha, back on her boulder, threw back her head and howled. Ralph, standing just below her, joined in. Soon howls echoed from all directions.

And it was beautiful.

Chapter Fourteen

Mrs. Righter dropped me off at Grandma's house to spend the night after we got back from the sanctuary. I knew Grandma wanted to hear all about our adventure, but I just couldn't put into words what it had been like. First to see Luna with the pups she adopted as her own, and then to see Ralph and Sascha—two rejects—find each other. It was . . . I don't know what it was.

So we spent a quiet evening, me watching *SpongeBob* and Grandma reading another smoochy book on the couch. The next morning, when Grandma took me home, she had to park in the street. Our driveway was jammed with cars, most of them—judging by stick figure family stickers, soccer bumper stickers, and stuffed animals peeking out of back-seats—mom vans.

"What's going on?" I asked Grandma.

"Oh, yeah," she said as she moved the gear stick to park. "Your mom told me about this. It's a moms' club."

"Moms have clubs?" I asked. "Why?"

Grandma shrugged. "To make friends and stuff. This one is for moms who have kids with . . . issues."

My hands felt clammy and my eyes suddenly felt like sweat was dripping into them. "Issues?" I whispered. "Ms. Drake called home once. It was *one* yelling incident. I don't have *issues*."

Grandma rolled her eyes. "Oh, you have issues," she said. "But that's not what I meant. This is a group for moms whose children have developmental problems."

"Like Down's?" I asked. Grandma nodded. Whew, this wasn't about me. It was about Molly. "Can I go in?"

"Well, you live here, don't you?" Grandma laughed. But I noticed she didn't take the key out of the ignition. She just sat there, waiting for me to get out.

"You're not coming in?" I asked.

"Nope, lots to do today. I'll see you Wednesday."

I slouched toward the house, dragging my overnight bag. Suddenly, I felt tired. I didn't feel up to facing a bunch of moms with issue children. I wished I were still hanging out with my best friend, watching wolf packs being created.

Then I realized—and it was enough to make me jerk to a stop—I just had called Sam my best friend. Best friend. *So long, Becky. Nice not knowing you.* I smiled and sort of skipped the rest of the way to the front porch.

I eased open the screen door, not wanting to disturb what I thought would be a super sad get-together. About a half-dozen moms sat on the floor of the living room, their talking, laughing, and clapping louder than the toddlers and babies wandering around the house. None of them noticed me come in. They were all so happy and chatty. Mom was right in the middle, sitting crisscross-applesauce. She was wearing lip gloss. I haven't seen her lips shiny in months. And she was smiling. Then she was laughing. And it wasn't an I've-made-a-decision-to-laugh type laugh. This was a real one, with one hand against her chest and her body folding over her legs. Molly squirmed in her other arm.

"Mom?" I gasped.

She looked up at me with a start. "Hey, Lucy!" she said, still chuckling. She handed Molly to the mom who had made her laugh and stood up. "We have some snacks in the kitchen if you're hungry. How was Grandma's? And the sanctuary?"

"Fine," I mumbled, feeling a little confused. The kitchen table was covered with plastic trays of food—cheese curls, brownies, chips, pretzels, cheese cubes, juice boxes, and soda cans. Talk about a snack jackpot! "Where did this come from?"

For weeks, the snacks in our house had been crackers and stale pretzels. Mom kept "meaning to go to the store" and then "running out of time." (Even though when I left for school in the morning, she was in sweatpants on the couch holding Molly and when I came back at the end of the day, she was in sweatpants on the couch holding Molly.)

"The other moms brought them," Mom said.

This moms' club thing was amazing! Mom was laughing, and I was eating good stuff. I grinned at her, and she grinned back. I started to fill a plate with goodies. That's when I noticed the little kids.

"That girl is holding Mr. Stinky!" I gasped, pointing to a toddler trudging through the kitchen slurping on a juice box. I gasped again when she wiped her sticky, cheese curl-stained fingers all over Mr. Stinky.

Mr. Stinky was once Mr. Teddy. That's when my special blanket with the teddy bear head still had his eyes and ears.

He also was yellow. Dad renamed him Mr. Stinky a few years ago when he began to look the way he does now—grayish brown and zombielike.

Mr. Stinky doesn't leave my bedroom anymore, but once I carried him everywhere under my arm like this kid was doing.

One time, when I was four, we spent the night in a hotel at the beach, and I left Mr. Stinky under the pillow. Did I mention that the beach is six hours from home? More than an hour into the drive back, I realized Mr. Stinky was gone. I cried so hard when Dad said he wouldn't go back for Mr. Stinky that I threw up. We went back.

"What is that girl doing with Mr. Stinky?" I gasped again.

"Oh," said Mom, smile fading. "I must've forgotten to lock your bedroom door."

Another kid walked by wearing six—six!—of my headbands. They draped down his forehead like a mask. "Ha!" he said as he ran by, arms outstretched toward another kid who screamed. "Ha!"

"Relax, Lucy," Mom said. "It's not like Mr. Stinky can't hold up under strain."

The girl put her juice box to Mr. Stinky's mouth (okay, the

line of stitching where he once had a mouth). She squeezed. Purple juice splotched his face.

"Mom!" I wailed.

She sighed and wove through the cluster of kids to the girl with Mr. Stinky. "I'm sorry, sweetie. I need to take this guy back. Maybe you'd like to get a different toy?"

The girl shook her head and squeezed my Mr. Stinky. Mom looked over at me. I glared as hard as I could. Mom sighed and gently pulled at Mr. Stinky.

"Mine!" the girl squealed.

I know it was dumb of me, but it was only then that I realized that all of the little kids had the same shaped eyes. Some of them wobbled a bit more than most kids. This little girl holding Mr. Stinky was probably Scrappy's age, but she seemed a lot younger. All of these kids had Down syndrome. Like Molly.

For a second, I felt something horrible and ugly twist inside, like my intestines had turned into snakes. I bit down on my lip to keep from crying out. They were so *different*. Molly was going to be like them and be this different, too. Those stares strangers gave Molly at the park—I realized I was looking at these kids the same way. Those stares would never go away. I scrunched my eyes shut because they were stinging again.

Mom thought I was just almost crying because of stupid Mr. Stinky. She tugged again on the bear blanket and the little girl cried.

"She can have him," I muttered.

Mom stared at me for a second and then handed Mr. Stinky back to the little girl, who smiled and hugged him tighter with her sticky fingers.

"Only for the play date," Mom assured me. "She won't take Mr. Stinky home with her."

I nodded and drifted toward Molly in the living room. That other mom—the one who had made Mom laugh so hard—was still holding her propped up against her chest. In front of the mom, the little boy with my headbands danced. The mom laughed again. I could tell from the way she did it that she was used to laughing. That she did it all the time. The little boy moved faster in his dance and laughed with her. He fell into her arms and she caught him, shielding Molly but hugging him back, too.

I walked over and held out my arms for my sister. Molly's arms waved and feet kicked when she saw me, and she smiled. The mom handed her to me, and I held her against my chest. For once, Mom didn't try to take her from me. She just sat down on the other side of the room. I felt her eyes on me, though.

I sat down, holding Molly face out and resting her against my stomach so she could watch the other kids. Headband boy plopped next to me, practically on my lap. A little truck was in front of him, so I rolled it over to him. He smiled and rolled it back to me. Soon we were crashing the truck into our knees. Other little kids sat down around us, adding a ball, a doll, and Mr. Stinky to the mix.

I thought I'd get bored in a second, but Molly's arms and legs went nutso whenever one of the toys came near her. She was having fun. And so was I.

The snakes stopped swirling in my stomach.

That night, Mom knocked softly on my bedroom door. She threw Mr. Stinky on my bed. "Fresh from the spa," she said. That's what she called it when she managed to get him into the washing machine. I usually pitched a fit when she tried to wash him.

I ran my fingers across the faint purple outline of juice across where his mouth once was. "Thanks."

Mom sat on my bed. "It was really nice of you to share

Mr. Stinky with Ashley today," she said.

"Her name's Ashley?"

Mom nodded.

"Will that club be coming around a lot?" I asked.

"I don't know," Mom answered. "I hope so. Would it be okay with you if they did?"

I hugged Mr. Stinky to my chest and nodded. "I like those kids," I said. "They seem happy." I bit my lip, then let more words spill from my mouth. "I hope Molly is happy."

Mom ran her fingers through my bangs. "She is. And she will be. So long as she has people who love her as much as we do, she has no reason not to be happy."

"She's not all that different from me, is she?" I said. "Not really, I mean."

"Sounds like you had an epiphany today." Mom laughed at my crooked eyebrow got-no-idea-what-you're-saying look. "It means you realized something important. You know what? I had the same epiphany."

Chapter Fifteen

"Aaarrooo!" I howled as Sam walked down the hall to meet me outside gym class.

"Woof," he muttered, looking around first to make sure no one from our class was around.

"Come on! Howl! We're a pack now, remember?" I bumped him in the shoulder.

"Do you think maybe you're taking this wolf thing a little too far?" Sam said.

I shrugged. The people streaming down the hall seemed to flow around us like we were an untouchable island. A lot of them stared at us and more than a few whispered loudly to each other as they passed. I didn't know who they were talking about more. Me or Sam. Two girls walked slower than necessary by us, whispering and giggling meanly as they did.

"Rouf!" I barked toward them like Sascha would.

They rushed away.

"What is wrong with you?" Sam stopped in place and stared at me.

"Nothing," I grinned. "I had a litany."

"You're not making any sense. And you're barking. Do you need to see the nurse?"

"A litany! It means realizing something important," I rolled my eyes at his lack of vocab and grabbed his arm so he would stop looking at all the people staring at us and just see me. "They see us as different. They're always going to see us as different. So what? We can be different together."

"Do you have a fever? How many fingers am I holding up?"

"Three." I stomped my foot. "Just listen, okay? We're freaks in this school. There's, like, no hope anymore. We're always going to be the girl who split her skirt while yelling and the boy who hung from his underpants in the locker room."

"Shut up," hissed Sam, his face a flaming tomato.

"Who cares?" I hissed back. "For some stupid reason, they feel better when they make us feel worse. So have a litany with me. Let's be different together. Let's be however we want. Let's be our own pack! I'll be Sascha. You be Ralph!" I let out another howl. (Maybe it was a bit much to howl again at the end.)

But I saw the corners of Sam's mouth quiver and his dimple flash for a second. He looked at his shoes and nodded. "Why do I have to be Ralph?" he muttered.

"Ralph is a noble name," I grunted in a pretty good Aunt Shelley imitation.

"Woof," he barked.

"You need to work on your bark or I'll stick with being a lone wolf here."

Feeling bold, I linked my arm through his. "Off to face the alphas!" We walked arm in arm to Ms. Drake's classroom.

I'd like to say that the rest of the day was great. I want to tell you that Sam and I smiled in the faces of everyone who whispered about us. It'd be nice to say that I didn't hear Becky's giggles or Tom calling me dog girl. And I'd like to say that Sam didn't duck his head whenever Henry walked past our desks, which was more than strictly necessary. (No one needs to visit the pencil sharpener six times an hour.)

But what I can say is that whenever someone did these things, we had each other. Sam rolled his eyes when Becky giggled and barked when Tom called me dog girl. (Sam really needs to work on the barking. He sounds like a tortured cat.) When Sam ducked his head, I raised mine higher and glared at Henry.

"That wasn't so bad," I said at our lunch table. "We present our wolf report in an hour, and then the day's practically over."

Sam nodded and separated his animal crackers into herds. I ate the buffalos. It seemed the most wolfish thing to do. *Maybe we* are *taking this wolf thing too seriously.*

Becky sauntered over to our table. She fluffed her perfect red curls and put her hand on her hip. Then she just stared at us. Sam glanced up at her and went back to his animal crackers. He mimed his lion animal cracker devouring his zebra, and I laughed, but not really.

Becky made a coughing noise.

Sam and I launched into an all-out zebra versus lion war. Animal cracker heads and limbs flew.

Becky coughed again.

Sam sighed and wiggled his eyebrows at me. I think that's his who's-going-to-ask-first look. I copied his sigh, then remembered that I was Sascha. I turned in my seat to face her and said, "What's up, Becky?"

She fluffed her curls again, glancing back at the "cool" table (I didn't follow her look, but I was sure Tom and Henry were watching). "Since your dad called my mom and told her I had to stop calling you at home, I thought I should let you know a few things in person."

"My dad did what?" I felt my zebra crumble in my hand, but Becky didn't stop her speech.

"First, we are *not* best friends any more. Here or anywhere. Now or ever."

Sam wiggled his eyebrows again and we both burst out laughing. This time for real.

"Sort of figured that, Becky," I said in a hiccup.

"Second, *everyone* in this *entire* school is making fun of you and your stupid little boyfriend."

Even though I was shaking and felt like I had to throw up, I leaned back in my chair. I stretched my legs out in front of me and draped my arms over the backrest. One of the wolf books from the library said when two wolves are about to fight, they each make themselves look as big as possible. I had seen Sascha do this while waiting to see if Ralph was a friend or enemy. I also remembered Miss Betsy saying martial artists always look their opponent in the eye. I knew I wasn't going to fight Becky, not with my hands or anything. But taking up more room and staring into her mean little eyes made me feel stronger. So did having Sam beside me.

"Sam and I are friends," I said, shocked at how calm my voice stayed. "You remember what it's like to have friends, don't you?"

Her overly glossy mouth fell open. "Seriously?" Becky crossed her arms and blinked at me a couple of times. She looked lost for a second. I think I wasn't allowing her speech go as planned. "Everyone likes *me*," she said. "*I* am by far the coolest girl in this school. Everyone wants to be my friend."

"Yeah," Sam said. "But who actually *is* your friend?"

Becky blinked a couple more times, her pale face blushing. I knew she hated blushing.

"I'm not here to talk to *you*." Her hands formed fists so hard her knuckles turned white. She glared at me. "You're making a fool out of yourself with all of this dog stuff. *Everyone* is making fun of you."

"Prepare yourself for a shock," I said. "But Tom and Henry aren't everyone." I heard Sheldon, who was sitting with April at the table behind us, snort. I suddenly realized that everyone around us had stopped eating and was listening.

Becky breathed so hard from her nose that she looked like a bull. "I'm not just talking about them," she snapped. "You guys are pathetic. Pathetic dorks. Forget dogs, okay? You can make a pack of dorks."

Sam and I smiled at each other. "We're way ahead of you. That's just what we were thinking," I said. "But just to be clear, we actually like wolves, not dogs, Becky."

"But if people who liked dogs wanted to join in, I would let them," Sam said.

"Cats, too, I guess," I joked, turning my back to Becky in the hope she'd just move on.

"But not ducks. I hate ducks," Sam said.

"No one hates ducks. Ducks are adorable," I said. "What's wrong with ducks?"

"I hate ducks," said Amanda from the table beside Sheldon and April's.

Sam kicked out a chair for Amanda, and she walked over, slouching into it. I think she really did hate ducks. She smiled at me, a super small one. She should smile more often.

Sheldon turned in his seat. "Hadrosaurids are duck

ancestors. They were much cooler than ducks, though. They could run faster than a T-Rex. I like hadrosaurids."

"Great. Hardrosaurids lovers are in. Want to sit with us, Sheldon?" Sam said.

"I like monkeys! Monkeys are cool!" April chirped.

"There you have it. You're in, too," I said, pulling out a chair for her.

Becky growled. The five of us laughed so hard we never heard her go back to her table. When the bell rang, she was sitting there with Tom and Henry, no one looking or talking to each other.

"I feel sort of bad for them," I whispered to my pack.

Sam shrugged. April smoothed her skirt. She spent a lot of time running her hands along her skirt like she didn't know what to do with her fingers now that she broke the nose-picking habit. Amanda's angry eyes flicked from our table to Tom's.

"We could just, you know, ignore them," Sheldon said.

"Ignoring everything makes me mad," Amanda snapped.

"Everything makes you mad," I pointed out. "Maybe you should work on that."

"They have their territory, we have ours," Sam said.

"Ever think you're taking this wolf thing too far?" I asked him.

Chapter Sixteen

Sam and I presented our class report on wolves at the end of the day. Technically, our reports were due earlier in the week, but Ms. Drake gave us an extension so we had time to work in our sanctuary trip.

For our diorama, Dad had helped me build a model of the sanctuary. I know it's sort of stupid, but I got chills when I added a black wolf to the pack with the red one representing Sascha. For the presentation, Sam and I took turns reading pages from our report, and then we were opened it up for questions.

Ms. Drake went first. "So, you've said wolves have a hierarchy. Which other social systems do you believe have an order, where there is a clear definition of who is in charge?"

Sam and I answered at the same time. He said, "The government" just as I blurted, "Middle school."

The class laughed. Ms. Drake asked Sam to elaborate. He said about how the senate, congress, and president are the alphas and the people the pack members.

When Ms. Drake turned to me, I added, "Our class has packs, too. There are some people who think they're alphas. People who think they can act however they want or do whatever they want because, for some reason, they act powerful. But real alpha wolves take care of the rest of the pack. They aren't just in charge in order to be cruel. Here, the kids who think they're the most popular, or the coolest, they're usually the biggest jerks."

Amanda whisper-shouted, "Yeah!" Sheldon nodded so hard his glasses slid down his nose. April twisted a tissue in her hands and glared at Becky. Ms. Drake's eyes narrowed and her arms crossed, but she didn't interrupt me.

"How do wolves handle an alpha who isn't doing a good job?" Ms. Drake asked.

"They form a new pack," Sam said.

When the bell rang, my pack gathered around the monkey bars.

"This might be the best day ever," said Sam, a smile spreading across his face. "We aced our report. We stood up to Becky. We're . . . we're just awesome."

I laughed. "I know what you mean! If I could do a back flip, I'd totally do one right now."

"Sam can! He can do a back flip!" April piped up.

And there, in front of everyone, Sam slipped off the monkey bars and did a flip in the grass. Amanda hooted, and Sheldon clapped. From the other side of the playground, Tom shouted, "Loser!"

Henry leaned from the top of the playscape, cupped his hands over his mouth, and shouted, "Watch it, Monkey Boy! You might find yourself hung up again!"

And just like that, Sheldon dropped down from the bars. He ripped off his jacket and growled so loud a vein in his neck popped. I've got to admit, the skinny kid looked freakishly strong. "Try it, numbskull! Just try it, and I'll go T-Rex on your butt!"

"Yeah," Amanda cracked her knuckles. "No one messes with our pack."

April and I moved simultaneously to stand beside Sam, glaring full force at Tom and Henry. April brought her fists up and bent her knees like she was about to spar in karate. Sam put his hand on my shoulder and howled. It still sounded like a tortured cat, but only until the rest of joined in.

Tom and Henry rolled their eyes, but they didn't come any closer.

When it was time to go back inside, I felt a soft tap on my shoulder. I turned to see Becky.

"I think we said all there is to say at lunch," I snapped.

"Look, all right," Becky stammered. "I was wrong. Tom and Henry are jerks. I thought Tom would want to be my boyfriend, but he told me I'm boring." She blinked at me with big eyes, like she really thought I'd feel sorry for her.

"And?" I said.

"And I was a jerk, too," she blurted. "I was wrong. I should've been a better friend. Now I don't have anyone." The tears in her eyes looked real. "Can you give me another shot?"

"Wow, Becky," I said. "You really would do anything to be popular. Even join a pack of dorks."

Becky's mouth twitched like she was fighting to keep a scream inside.

"What do you guys think?" I asked Sam and April, who were not at all subtle about listening in from their spots in line ahead of me.

"Room for anyone, right?" April asked.

Sam laughed. "That's right. But maybe we'll just pretend you're not in the pack. You know, Becky, so we can find out what everyone else thinks of you first."

"Gawd! Forget it!" Becky stamped her foot and stormed to the back of the line.

"Beck!" I called. "Why don't you call me later? We can talk, all right? And go from there. I'll let my dad know it's cool for you to call me again." She paused and nodded without turning around.

Sam bumped me with his shoulder. "You're nicer than you ought to be."

I bumped him back. "I've got to be nice. My pack depends on me."

Acknowledgments

For loving me more than I deserve, thank you to my husband. Jon always introduced me as a writer, years before I felt like one, and he never stopped supporting my dream. His confidence and encouragement made this possible.

Thank you also to Emma and Benny, for inspiring me every day. Being your mother is the best, most important part of my life.

I am honored to be represented by Nicole Resciniti of The Seymour Agency. Nicole, thank you for believing in me and sticking with me. In addition to being incredible at what you do, you've created an amazing support system of clients and friends. I'm thrilled to be a member.

To my amazing editor Julie Matysik, thank you doesn't

begin to scratch the surface of my gratitude. I'm blessed to work with you.

Thank you to my mom, who read my first ever story and told nine-year-old me, "This should be published." Dad, you helped me see wonderful stories—and a lot of humor—in everyday life. Thank you for that. Amy and Michele, thank you for cheering me on.

Much love also goes to Buffy Andrews for never letting me give up on my dream and sharing the tools I needed to achieve it. I couldn't ask for a better mentor and friend.

Q&A with Beth Vrabel

Q: Where do you get your ideas for your books?

BV: Ideas come from anywhere and everywhere. That's why I'm sure to keep a notebook nearby at all times—just in case.

Q: When did you know you wanted to be a writer?

BV: I wrote my first story just for me—not because it was an assignment for school—when I was nine years old. I remember my mom reading it and saying, "One day you'll get published." I could picture it, that little story I wrote, on shelves.

You know, looking back on that now, I can't help but wonder what would've happened if Mom had just said, "That's nice, Beth," and moved on to whatever else she had been doing before I waved those pages in her face. Maybe I would've fallen in love with writing on my own. Maybe I wouldn't have.

The thing that strikes me is the power of that moment of kindness on my mom's part. It didn't cost her anything—maybe a few minutes—to read those pages, smile, and encourage me. But it changed the course of my life. I try to be mindful of that now as a mom but also as a person who spends a lot of time with children. One moment of kindness and attention can be so powerful.

Q: What gave you the idea to write this book?

BV: I think we all go through a period where we feel a little picked on and misunderstood. For me, that was fourth grade. My dad had been seriously injured at work, with a long recovery period. He and Mom were understandably stressed and distracted. While I didn't completely understand what they were dealing with, I knew not to bring up things, like that other kids were laughing at my penny loafers, to them. All my buddies from third grade seemed to have paired up with new friends during the summer, and I felt pretty alone. I remember searching the cliques in my classroom, trying to find a place where I fit. It's a lonely feeling, but powerful material for a future writer!

Q: Are you a lot like Lucy?

BV: Oh, I wish! While Lucy might not be the nicest, most considerate person, she is authentic. I wish I had known and respected myself as much as her by the time I finished fourth grade. I wallowed. Lucy takes action!

Q: How long did it take to write *Pack of Dorks*?

BV: I've got a short and a long answer to this question. Here's the short version: About a year. I wrote most of *Pack of Dorks* at a local coffee shop while my son was in preschool.

Now, for the long version, I'd say it took me about five years and four books. Even though *Pack of Dorks* is my first published book, it's not the first I've written. My first novel, I'll just say it, was terrible. So, so bad that kittens died. For real! I wanted to write a Serious Work of Fiction. You know, those books that make you think and hurt and long. That was the type of book I was certain I should be writing. Well, it didn't take long to realize instead of a Serious Work of Fiction, I had just written a dull, depressing book.

But here's the thing: I had finished a whole novel! Sure, no one, aside from my ever-loving mom and sisters, would read it, but I finished it. And that meant I could do it again.

The next time, I tried writing the kind of book I loved to read. It was full of excitement and drama and even a little magic. I liked the story when it was finished, but I knew it wasn't great. Why? It didn't read like a story I would write. It read like a story I wrote to sound like other writers. Does that make sense?

But once again, I had finished. And that meant I could do it again. This time, I wrote a story only I could tell. I shared it the way I would tell a friend a story. I love that novel, and so did my friend and agent, Nicole, but publishers didn't agree that it was ready for bookshelves.

I didn't give up. I sat down and wrote again. This time, *Pack of Dorks*. And you know what? It was so fun to write. I cracked myself up as I typed in the coffee shop. I teared up, too, during certain scenes. When I was done, I was so proud because I knew this was a story only I could create.

Q: Where's your favorite place to write?

BV: I have three. The first is for when I'm home alone. Then I put on HGTV and write while sitting on the couch, preferably with a cup of coffee in my favorite mug and a box of Girl Scout cookies. My second favorite is in the summer, when I write on our deck next to a little pond. My children are usually playing in the woods surrounding our yard, so in between the croaks of the frogs in the pond, I hear them as they scurry up trees and explore the wilderness. The third is the coffee shop in town. My daughter, who also loves to write, brings her laptop, too. We'll sit side by side, me with my coffee (black, thank you) and her with her smoothie (vanilla bean), and write. She jokes that it's quality time with Mom, where we basically ignore each other for hours. The key to a good writing place seems to be a lot of background noise!

Q: Why did you decide to include Down syndrome as part of the story?

BV: It's important to me that books—especially books for young readers—include diversity. Many families face unexpected challenges, the way Lucy's family does when Molly is born with Down syndrome. When things like this happen, families need time to adjust. Maybe they're even sad and mournful for a time, but then they realize they're stronger and more capable than they thought. I love that impulsive, self-centered Lucy is the one to prove this to her parents.

Q: What scares you?

BV: Spiders, falling, and fevers.

Q: What is a dork?

BV: To me, a dork is someone who isn't like everyone else and doesn't try to be. Too many of us spend too much time trying to fit in, to be like everyone else, when what we really want is to stand out. Celebrate what sets you apart! Be a dork!

Take a peek at Beth Vrabel's next book,

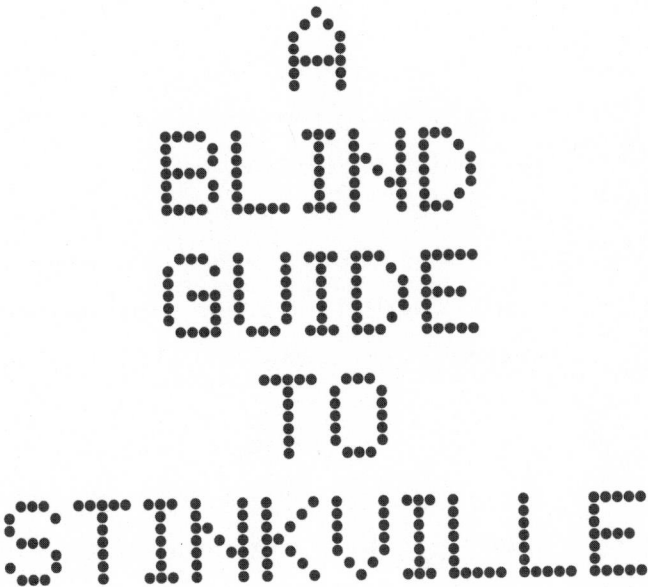

Available October 2015 from Sky Pony Press

Chapter One

Even *I could* see that Tooter was no Seeing Eye dog.

The ancient Shih Tzu was about the size of a loaf of bread. His bottom teeth poked out of his mouth all the time. His eyes were once brown but now they were sort of gray. Tooter's favorite thing in the world to do was to rub his butt against the ground. Or the table. Or someone's leg. And to fart. And that's the story behind the name Tooter.

After Mom finally agreed that my brother, James, could walk me to the library instead of making me spend another summer day alone at home (I mean, I guess, technically, it's home, even though it doesn't feel like it yet), he grabbed Tooter's leash from a hook by the door.

"Come on, Alice. Might as well take care of two needy pains-in-the-butt," he muttered.

We moved to Sinkville, South Carolina, about three months ago. Sinkville is the official name, but everyone calls it *Stink*ville.

Home, I mean *real* home, is Seattle, Washington. We lived there, right along the shore, all twelve years of my life. There was always a wonderful blanket of soft gray in the sky, so I only had to put on sunscreen once in the morning and my milk-white skin stayed perfectly pale. The air smelled salty and like rain. Mom would walk me to school during the school year, and I'd spend the summer hanging out with my best friend, Eliza, who lived a block from us. Her mom let her walk over to our house by herself in the morning, but of course it was impossible for me to head out on my own. So we'd always hang out at my home. Mom would bake us cookies and tell us stories about her life B.A. (before Alice), when she was a travel writer. She made every day feel like an adventure. Sometimes when Dad came home from work, he'd say, "Where'd ya go today, Alice?" And I'd say anything from Argentina to Zaire, wherever Mom had talked about that day.

Here in Stinkville, life is pretty much the opposite of before. We live in a little house in the middle of the woods. Even with all the trees, the sky is blazing blue. I have to put on sunscreen every other hour. For real. And the air in Stinkville? It smells like rotting eggs. That's because the whole town is centered on M. H. Bartel Paper Mill, where almost everyone (including the new plant manager, a.k.a. my dad) in town works.

Do you know how paper is made? I don't either. But I do know it involves purposefully rotting wood. Rotting wood emits incredibly horrible smells. The scariest part: no one in town even smells it anymore. For real. So if we live in Stinkville long enough we'll get used to the stink and we won't even know how horrible it is to new people!

And if that wasn't stinktastic enough, Mom doesn't walk me to school or anywhere for that matter. Mostly that's because we moved in the summer, so there *is* no school. But also because the longer we live here, the less Mom does anything Momish. She took me to the library the first week we were here but has been "too tired," "feeling a little overwhelmed," or "grrrmmlll" (the approximate sound she makes when I nudge her awake), since. She doesn't even tell me to brush my teeth any-more, let alone explain what happened when she went diamond mining in Tanzania years ago.

But what about hanging out all day with my BFF? Well, she's literally across the country. And I'm here. With no friends. No life. My only excitement now is going to M. H. Bartel Public Library (yup, even the library was named after the paper mill).

When James, Tooter, and I got to the library doors, I stomped and refused to go inside without my brother.

"What is your deal?" he hissed. "I said I'd take you to the library, not hold your books for you."

"I can't go by myself." I stomped again.

"Why not?"

I glared at him.

"Are you playing the blind card?" he sighed.

"I'm not playing," I snapped. "I'm actually blind. And you have to help me."

"I don't have to do anything," James snapped back. But he looked around for someplace to tie Tooter's leash.

"Do you think it's okay to leave him out here?" I muttered. I mean, it was about a thousand degrees out. Under my enormo sunhat, my sweaty hair felt wet, as if I had just left the shower. Tooter's little pink tongue hung out of his mouth and almost touched the sidewalk.

"Urgh!" James jerked open the door to the library and stepped in, dragging Tooter along by the leash.

The cool fresh air hit my face as we walked inside and I breathed as deeply as I could. My glasses turn to sunglass lenses when I'm outside, so for a minute I was even more blind than usual while the lenses adjusted.

"Excuse me!" a high-pitched voice that seemed to come out of the speaker's nose rather than her mouth called out. "We do not allow animals in here. This. Is. A. Library!"

As my lenses transitioned, I could make out a huge desk in front of us. Behind it, I saw a bright red blur that I think was the speaker's shirt and a fluffy mound of yellow, which had to be her hair.

"I'm sorry," James said. "It's just, I'm bringing my sister here. I had to actually bring her in because she's blind . . ."

"Oh!" The librarian sucked in her breath. I went ahead and rolled my eyes, figuring the person behind the desk was a) Not looking at me, and b) Not able to see behind my dark lenses anyway.

Where we used to live, everyone knew I was blind. It wasn't a big deal. It was accepted, the same way everyone accepted that Josh's mom always was last to pick him up from playdates and that Eliza's hair was too curly to lie flat around her face.

But here, being blind is news. And this is the way it goes when people find out about me: they gasp. Then, if I'm close enough, I'll see this awful expression on their faces, like they just ate some bad cheese but are holding it in their mouths instead of spitting it out. Then they become overly helpful, usually asking the person I'm with what they can do to help instead of asking me. They also speak super loudly, like maybe I'm also deaf. No one ever asks *me* questions.

If they did, I'd be able to explain.

So you've heard of 20/20 vision being normal? I'm 20/200 in my left eye, 20/210 in my right. So a "normal" person could read something from two hundred feet away that I'd have to be twenty feet from in order to read. I know, I know. You're making the bad cheese face for me. Please stop. The point is: I can read. I just have to be really close.

Soon after making the gaspy voice, the librarian came out from behind the desk. My lenses were clearing up. She stood way too close to me, so I could make out that her lipstick was gloppy and pink, and that her yellow hair was gray at the roots. She smelled like lavender mixed with a little rotting eggs. I wonder if that was the paper mill stink on her.

"I am Mrs. Dexter," the librarian said, slowly and loudly.

James snickered beside me, quickly turning it into a cough.

"I'm Alice," I answered.

She stared hard at my eyes, which made me nervous. And that, in turn, made my eyes move faster. So I guess I should just go ahead and say it. I'm blind because I have albinism. You know, like an albino. It just means my skin is about the color of paper, my hair is, too, and my eyes are blue. Everyone who has albinism is visually impaired. We have something called nystagmus, which makes our eyes always move back and forth. A lot of albinos aren't blind like me, though; they are just visually impaired.

"Service animals are welcome in the M. H. Bartel Library, as are any individuals with special needs. Welcome, Alice." Mrs. Dexter said all of this with long. Pauses. Between. Each. Word. "Welcome," she said again.

James now openly grinned at me. He handed me Tooter's leash. The dumb dog was scooting his butt along the carpet but seemed a little peppier in the air-conditioned building.

"Text me when you're ready for me to pick you up," James said. The traitor turned to leave.

"Wait!" Mrs. Dexter stole my line. "Does the Seeing Eye dog know where the large print section is or do I need to tell it?"

"Oh, he'll figure it out," James answered, and all three of us looked down at Tooter, who took the opportunity to sniff his own butt with one stubby leg in the air. "Just let Tooter dig right in."

"Well, Tooter," Mrs. Dexter patted Tooter's head. "Let me know if you need anything."

"Where's the children's section?" I asked.

Mrs. Dexter seemed surprised that I spoke. "It's to the left." Tooter glanced up at her, so she pointed in that direction. "But we don't have Braille children's books here . . ."

"Actually, I can read," I said, walking purposefully to the left. "I just need to get closer." And I think it all would've made a good impression on Bad Cheese Face Librarian had I not tripped.

Ah! The children's section. I stopped at the entranceway and breathed in the smell of books and chaos. From the back of the vast room, I heard giggles and chattering as a preschool program let out. Beside me to the right, tables were set up. And all in front of me, rows and rows and rows of books. Someday I'm going to have a library in my own house. I think I could go ahead and skip the living room and just put in a reading room, with piles of books where the television should be.

Tooter pushed ahead of me and jumped onto a chair that was shaped like an open hand. I scooped him up and sat down in his place, holding him to my lap. The chair was pretty cool but it felt a little strange to be leaning back on a thumb. I reached out, grabbed a book at random, and opened it. I think I would've read the dictionary at that point; I was just so happy to be someplace comfortable. And, just so you know, I can read regular books. I just have to hold the book a couple inches from my face and hope there aren't italics. Nystagmus makes a mess of italics. I use a magnifier to help me read, too.

It's small and sort of looks like a credit card, so I simply keep it in my back pocket.

"Um, you're not actually allowed to bring pets in here." I glanced over the cover of the book, which ended up being *Because of Winn-Dixie*, in the direction of the voice. "That's the rule, even if you are reading a dog book."

In front of me was a girl about my age, maybe eleven or twelve. Her arms were crossed and her voice was super quiet, maybe because we were in a library, but mostly she seemed like the type to always have a quiet voice.

She leaned forward to rub Tooter's fluff-ball head. The girl's dark brown skin made my milky white skin look even more like Oreo stuffing. Tooter tilted his head into her hand and let his tongue roll out of his open mouth. "Kate DiCamillo, the author of your book, writes that it's hard not to fall in love with a dog with a great sense of humor," she said with a slight laugh.

"He's my Seeing Eye dog," I said.

The girl laughed. "Sure he is."

I smiled back. "The lady up front fell for it. So now Tooter is here . . ."

"Mrs. Dexter isn't all there, you know what I mean?" The girl twirled her finger next to her ear and then sat in the other hand chair next to mine. "I'm Kerica, by the way. My mom's the children's librarian. She's going to freak when she sees your dog in here. I want a dog so bad, but she keeps saying no."

"I'm Alice. I just moved here a few weeks ago."

"I figured," Kerica said. "It's a small town. Someone new sticks out."

"They stand out even more if they're an albino."

Kerica snorted. Then she bit her lip and smashed her lips together so hard that I snorted, too. "I'm sorry!" she gasped. "I didn't mean to laugh. But it was just so—"

"Obvious?" I laughed. Soon we were both giggling.

In just a few minutes, I learned a lot of things. First, Kerica spends every summer day, all day, in the library with her mom. She's read about forty books already and it was only the end of June!

"Most of them are dog books," she said, and shrugged in a sad sort of way, which I immediately got. Everyone knows dog stories are a downer. "When I'm tired of reading, I draw pictures of the characters." She flipped open the notebook she was holding and held it up for just a second. I pretended I could see the drawing.

Second, Kerica asks direct questions but they don't feel rude. Like when she asked me if everyone in my family has albinism (nope, just me) and then said, "That must feel a little lonely." That could've made me feel sad, but it didn't. It made me feel like she understood.

"Is that a dog in my library?" a booming voice called out.

Kerica kept on rubbing Tooter's head, who had abandoned my lap for hers the second Kerica had sat down. "Simmer down, Ma. It's a Seeing Eye dog."

Kerica's mom stood in front of me, her arms crossed. She looked so much like a bigger, softer version of Kerica that I had to smile. She watched the two of us for a long moment. "Does Mrs. Dexter know about this animal in here?"

I nodded. "If it helps, I really am blind."

"She's got albinism, Ma."

"'S'at right?" She muttered in the slow southern twang I was still getting used to hearing. She seemed a little caught off guard, but didn't have the bad cheese face.

It's kind of funny. When I lived in Seattle, everyone I knew had always known me. Like Eliza and I had been in the same playgroup when we were babies. Our neighbors had never moved. My elementary school teachers had all taught James before me. Everyone knew everything about me without my ever having to tell them. So I had never had to explain albinism, blindness, or nystagmus to anyone before. They already knew.

But here I was in this library for less than an hour, and I already had to tell three people I was blind. This third time it just sort of slipped out.

"Ma, this is Alice. She's new to town," Kerica said.

"Welcome, Alice. I'm Mrs. Morris. Make sure your dog doesn't do-do in the library." Mrs. Morris started to walk away, then turned back suddenly and rubbed Tooter's head. This was seriously the dog's best day ever.

Honestly, it was *my* best day ever in Stinkville, too.